Sundance #36

TRAIL DRIVE

Peter McCurtin

LEISURE BOOKS ∞ NEW YORK CITY

A LEISURE BOOK

Published by

Nordon Publications, Inc.
Two Park Avenue
New York, N.Y. 10016

Copyright © 1981 by Nordon Publications, Inc.

All rights reserved
Printed in the United States

Two Fists Against Four

The Pendletons had stripped down to pants and boots; Sundance took off his hat and shirt. The Irishman stared at the old scars criss-crossing Sundance's belly and chest. Some had been made by bullets and knives; most were the result of his boyhood initiation into Cheyenne warriorship.

Sundance knew he had to keep them in front of him, if he could. But he knew that wouldn't be possible all the time. Con was bigger and stronger than Frank, but Frank was faster on his feet, and maybe more vicious. To Con, it was just another brawl; Frank, for his part, would fight like a wildcat because Molly was there.

"Come and get it, boss," Frank said, beckoning to Sundance.

Sundance stayed where he was and the instant they began to move he saw they fought as a team. Frank on the right, his brother on the left. Waiting for them to close in, Sundance tensed and then relaxed. To win, you had to believe in your brain and gut that you could do it. No, it was more than that: you had to will yourself to win, you had to push aside all doubt. There was no conceit in this, simply iron-willed determination. In the great fighting days of the Cheyenne he has been taught this by the fiercest fighter of all, Spotted Pony, who had taught him to show no fear—and no mercy.

We will send you a free catalog on request. Any titles not in your local book store can be purchased by mail. Send the price of the book plus 50¢ shipping charge to Leisure Books, P.O. Box 270, Norwalk, Connecticut 06852.

Titles currently in print are available for industrial and sales promotion at reduced rates. Address inquiries to Nordon Publications, Inc., Two Park Avenue, New York, New York 10016, Attention: Premium Sales Department.

The SUNDANCE Series

- No. 1 Overkill
- No. 2 Dead Man's Canyon
- No. 3 Dakota Territory
- No. 4 Death in Lava
- No. 5 The Pistoleros
- No. 6 The Bronco Trail
- No. 7 The Wild Stallions
- No. 8 Bring Me His Scalp
- No. 9 Taps at Little Big Horn
- No. 10 The Ghost Dancers
- No. 11 The Comancheros
- No. 12 Renegade
- No. 13 Honcho
- No. 14 War Party
- No. 15 Bounty Killer
- No. 16 Run for Cover
- No. 17 Manhunt
- No. 18 Blood on the Prairie
- No. 19 War Trail
- No. 20 Riding Shotgun
- No. 21 Silent Enemy
- No. 22 Ride the Man Down
- No. 23 Gunbelt
- No. 24 Canyon Kill
- No. 25 Blood Knife
- No. 26 The Nightriders
- No. 27 Death Dance
- No. 28 The Savage
- No. 29 Day of the Halfbreeds
- No. 30 Los Olvidados
- No. 31 The Marauders
- No. 32 Scorpion
- No. 33 Hangman's Knot
- No. 34 Apache War
- No. 35 Gold Strike

Chapter One

Sundance knew the word was out on him the minute he hit Brownsville. Blank stares greeted him as he rode into the South Texas town just across the Rio Grande from Mexico. On the other side of the Rio, wide and tidal and no longer muddy at this point, was the brawling Mexican town of Matamoros. He could smell the salt air from the Gulf; the air was full of sun and salt and a sense of danger. Well, he thought, it had to get out sooner or later; no way to keep a herd of three thousand cattle a secret. Still, the curious or hostile stares that followed him were a sure sign that they had known about it for a long time. Yet he would have been just as glad if the secret had leaked out later than sooner.

The railroad depot was on the edge of town; he was glad to be done with the long train ride from Washington. He didn't like the stink and bustle and noise of trains, but they were the only way to travel a long distance in the shortest time. And Sundance was in a hurry to get started. Once the herd was on the move there would be no hurry at all, for there was no way to hurry a cow. A cow walked or ran and if you wanted to keep the fat on you let the cow walk. There would be plenty of running by the time they got to Montana; few trail herds got through without at least one stampede. It was early April now and Montana was where he was going; the summer would be just about over by the time they got there. Before they reached Montana they would have crossed the United States from one end to the other. It was a journey to make a man think.

Sundance knew this would be no ordinary trail for his mission was far from ordinary, just as he himself was no ordinary man. The men who stared at him as he rode into Brownsville seemed to know who he was, as if they had been waiting for him to show up. But they could have no real knowledge of what he was. Few men did.

Sundance had long grown accustomed to the hostility that faced him wherever he went. He did nothing to foster this antagonism, minding his business as best he could, yet it was always there. There was something about him that caused lesser men to become uneasy, and by itself his very appearance would have been enough. He was tall, very tall, and rangy, dressed in buckskins from the top of his flat-crowned hat to his moccasined feet. His skin was the color of an old penny, his shoulder-length hair the color of new wheat. Set against the dark brown of his skin, his hard eyes were a startling blue. Light blue and far seeing, ever wary but not unfriendly. From his beaded weapons belt were slung a long-barreled Colt .44, a straight-handled throwing hatchet, and a thick-bladed Bowie knife that stopped just short of being the biggest fighting knife they made. The Bowie was a short sword rather than a knife, and its razor sharp blade with its heavy backing could sever a man's arm in a single blow.

Over his shoulder was the great ash bow with its quiver of steel-tipped arrows. The powerful bow always got the most attention from strangers, and more than anything else, even more than the dark color of his skin, it reminded him that he was half Indian. Half Cheyenne, his mother's people. The bow told people that for all his well mannered speech he was still half savage. This was true and Sundance himself knew it was true. He was what he was; for years now he had made peace with himself.

For all the hostility that greeted him no one dared to get in his way, and even the town children who like as not jeered at any stranger were silent. But they watched, as did their grown-up kin—everyone watched, waiting to see what he would do.

Brownsville, being a border town, had a Mexican part, and that's where he went. He knew the town, had been through it many times on his journeys south to many places in the past.

The adobe building that now housed the big cantina known as the Benito Cafe was older than the State of Texas. In this section of town he was less of a stranger, not that he was known to the Mexicans who lived there. It was simply because the color of a man's skin, or his appearance, didn't concern the Mexicans very much. If a man proved himself to be a man of honor then he was welcome.

Sundance dismounted, hitched his great stallion Eagle, though there was no need. The big intelligent horse was perfectly trained and would stand patiently until needed.

"Easy boy," Sundance told the stallion. "We'll be gone from this place before long."

Inside, the cantina was dark and cool after the sun-bright glare of the street. The smells of a century had soaked into its mud and stone and seasoned timbers. Dark wood like everything else, the bar ran the length of the place; there a few early morning drinkers lounged with glasses of beer or tequila or mescal in front of them. They stirred when he walked in, and so did the bartender, but being Mexican they were too polite to stare. But they watched him in the dust streaked mirror or through hooded eyes. They all knew why he had come; of what he had come to do. And like so many things about Sundance, it had not been done before.

The bartender came down the long bar. "Yes *senor*?" he said.

Sundance said he was looking for Don Francisco Aldama. "My name is Sundance. I was to meet him here today."

The bartender responded to Sundance's name as if he hadn't heard it before. That was polite. "Yes," he said in English. "He is waiting for you in the back room."

Sundance knocked and was told to come in. Francisco Aldama, still rail thin at seventy-five, stood up easily for a man of his years and clapped Sundance lightly on the arm with his left hand. The old man's right hand was sliding a .45 pistol back into its holster.

Sundance nodded at the now holstered pistol and smiled. "You think it's that dangerous, do you?"

They shook hands heartily and Sundance sat down. Two other men were at the table and they nodded. "Not so much for me," Francisco

Aldama said. "The real danger is for you. News of your coming is all over town." He turned to the two men, told them to wait at the bar.

Sundance poured a trickle of brandy into a glass. "It didn't come from me, Francisco. I know it didn't come from you. You have to remember that Washington is just a small town that looks like a city. You have the herd ready to cross?"

Francisco Aldama nodded. "I have been ready for days. You sure you want to go through with this, my friend? I am a rich man and can wait to sell the herd to someone else."

Sundance knew that Francisco Aldama would have to take a loss if he hung onto the herd. At first there would be no buyers at all. They would make him wait—their way of reminding him that he shouldn't have business dealings with a notorious halfbreed, a man who was hated by so many whites because he didn't conform to their idea of what a halfbreed should be.

It was good brandy, strong yet mellow, not that Sundance cared much for alcohol of any kind. Years before, he had learned in the most painful way that he couldn't handle it. Back in the days before he stopped drinking he had been truly a wild Indian. Nowadays, his limit was two drinks and no more. Occasionally, to ease the tensions of his dangerous life, he smoked a little marijuana, the rank Mexican weed that brought peaceful feelings for a while.

"You sold the herd to me, Francisco," Sundance said.

The old Mexican shrugged. "A way out, that's all I was offering."

"I don't want it, I want that herd," he replied.

"You have thought it over carefully?"

"Oh yes. I have considered all the possibilities."

"I think they will try to stop you."

"They may try. It depends how hard."

"You are a brave man, Sundance. The very thought of it stirs my blood."

Sundance shook his head. "Not brave, Francisco. You don't have to be brave when you know how to get things done. This is something I have to do in memory of my mother. No, that's not entirely true. I would do it anyway. The Cheyenne need that herd and I'm going to take it to them. Now they have little meat or no meat at all. What they have is often rancid, cut from cows that should have gone to the glue factory. It's rotten or diseased and the children get sick. The Cheyenne eat it because it's all they have to eat—and the Indian Ring continues to get rich."

Francisco Aldama sighed. "Such men!" he said. "Why can't they steal just enough to get fat?"

"They've stolen millions from the Indians," Sundance said. "They want to make more millions. It's that simple."

"I am surprised they haven't tried to stop you in some legal way." It was clear that the old Mexican had little respect for legality.

Sundance poured another small drink. "They tried but"—he smiled—"I have a powerful friend."

Francisco Aldama smiled too. "Yes, General Crook. He has been a good friend to you."

"And to the Indians," Sundance said. "When I started out to buy your herd and take it to the Cheyenne, the Ring put pressure on the Interior Department to stop me. They went to the Secretary and put pressure on him. Then they got their top man to go to the President himself. Crook blocked them both times. Grant may be a thickhead but he isn't a crook. He just doesn't know how to pick his friends. Even so, they were getting close to persuading him when Crook came roaring in. Even the President listens when George Crook roars. He reminded Grant of their days together during the War." Sundance smiled again. "The General admits it was blackmail—good blackmail, white blackmail, he called it. The President ordered the Secretary of the Interior to let me go ahead. The Customs men are to allow the herd to come across without any charge."

"How this Ring must hate you!" For an old man Francisco Aldama was a hearty drinker. His faded eyes glittered with satisfaction. "It is good to stand up to greedy men who think they have all the power. I am glad to help you in this."

"You gave me a fair price," Sundance said.

"As fair as I could make it. If one can not help an old friend, then what use is any of it?"

Sundance smiled. Don Francisco pretended the serenity of age, but he hated being old. Unlike most Mexicans, he was of pure Spanish blood. His father had been an officer in the old Spanish army, his mother a famous beauty from Castile. He had the blue eyes of Castile; the years had faded their color. Now his eyes were fierce, as if remembering the wild days of his youth.

"I would go with you, if I may," he said almost shyly. "Don't tell me I'm an old man, Sundance. There are some truths a man does not like to hear."

"With respect, Francisco, you are an old man,"

Sundance said. "You have grown old with honor. There is no longer any need to prove anything."

Francisco Aldama knocked back a glass of brandy. "Wait until you're old before you say that. Before my wife died I was happy enough to be old. We were both old but we didn't feel old. You know what I'm talking about?"

"Maybe I do."

"Then you don't know. I am not so old that I can't sit a horse all day. I can still shoot a gun." The old man smiled. "Not as good as you perhaps. I say perhaps. You think differently?"

Sundance said no. True, Francisco Aldama was old but the wildness remained in him. Well into his later years he had been a champion rider and a crack shot. To build his great hacienda it had been necessary to be both. In the past, many men had died in front of his gun.

"But what about your ranch?" Sundance asked. "If you join me you'll be on the trail for more than five months. That's a long time to be away, the way things can happen in your country."

"At my age it's a very long time," Francisco Aldama said, smiling and drinking. "Don't say yes because you think I can bring my vaqueros. I can bring a few. My son will need the others to take care of the rancho. As you say, things can happen fast in Mexico, and I have many enemies, as what rich man has not. All you get is me, Sundance."

"You're plenty."

The old man's face hardened, suspecting that he was being humored. "If you don't want me, all you have to do is say it. Our deal remains firm and we will part the friends we have been."

Sundance knew the old man thought he was

speaking the the truth. There would be resentment if he said no. The old man's offer had come as a surprise, a welcomed surprise. He didn't want to say no. He hadn't seen Francisco Aldama for five years, yet he looked as tough and wiry as ever. Only one thing remained to be settled and it was important to get it done here and now.

"I would be honored to have you along," Sundance said in Spanish. "But now we must speak of leadership. All your life you have given other men orders. On this drive you must take them—from me. You think you can learn to do that? No drive can have two leaders."

"Gently and truthfully spoken," the old man said. "You do not have to remind me, Sundance. It was in my mind before I decided. Yes, I can take orders—from you! You don't have to remind me now. In the days to come you may have to refresh your memory."

"You can count on that," Sundance said, smiling at the terrible tempered old man. "When you forget I'll be there to remind you."

"*Gracias*," Francisco Aldama said. "I shall remain forever in your debt."

They laughed and the old man had a drink on it. Sundance didn't.

"You have signed on other men?" Francisco Aldama asked, seeming to know that Sundance had not.

Sundance said, "I was hoping to do it here. There was a chance the Ring would ease back once the Secretary had given his permission. I see I was wrong. The bad feeling here is like a fog."

"A killing fog like that of a swamp," the old man said. "For a herd of this size you will need, would you say, fifteen men? About fifteen, including a horse wrangler and a cook."

"We can do it with maybe ten or twelve men. Make it twelve. You will be my *segundo*. I'll double as foreman and wrangler."

Francisco Aldama agreed that a smaller number of men than usual could do it, if they had to. "I was a *segundo* before I was a foreman. A good cook is most important."

"A good bad cook," Sundance said. "There are no good good cooks in the cow business."

"A cook no worse than the rest," Francisco Aldama said. "I cannot bring the cook I have. There would be insurrection. As you say, he cooks for my men in the right degree of badness. But a cook we must have. You think you can find one in Brownsville? Cooks of experience are sought eagerly, can name their own wages within reason."

"It won't be easy," Sundance said. Cooks, for all their ill temper and surliness, were the aristocrats of the range. They cooked and that's all they did. They didn't have to stand guard like the rest of the men. They didn't do any chores other than their own. You ate what they gave you—within reason, as Francisco would say—and if you didn't like it you could go and find yourself another cook. At best they were difficult men; in their worst moments they were tyrants. Cooks were a fact of life in the cow trade, and no one had ever been able to change it. An army marched on its stomach, and a trail herd was no different.

"I'll have to look around," Sundance said. "How many vaqueros can you give me?"

Francisco Aldama said no more than three. "My son will fight to give me that many. Vaqueros aren't like your cowboys, drifting from job to job. Most of my men have been with me for years. That's why my son will complain."

"Will he complain about you?"

"Only about the men. He knows better than to question what I do in personal matters. He is a good man but more a businessman than a *ranchero*. So he will see the loss of the men as bad business." The old man's mouth twisted in mild contempt. "Most of the fighting was over by the time my son was born."

So he doesn't get along with his son, Sundance thought. That had to be part of the reason he was coming along. The reason didn't matter. Old though he was, Francisco Aldama was still worth three men. Whatever happened, he would stand like a rock, fearless and implacable. Sundance wasn't sure that Francisco Aldama didn't hope to die a violent death on this drive. One way or another, it had to be his last. An old man with a wish to die could make for problems, Sundance knew, but everything in its own time.

"You will want to talk to your son," Sundance said. "I'll come across as soon as I round up some kind of crew." For now that was the real problem, finding men to go along with him. He knew he couldn't be too choosy, so he had to be careful. They were going to have to make it with a tight outfit; once a man was signed on and the herd was moving, he wouldn't be easy to replace. You could fire a man but it was hard to replace him. Sometimes you had to kill a man who wouldn't stand for being fired. There were times when you had to do it to keep the others in line. But it made for bad feeling, no matter how pressing the need or serious the offense that caused it to be done. It was natural for the men to stand together against the boss. Even men who didn't like one another would take sides against the boss. On a drive the men bunked together in their blankets, so if you killed one you had to be ready to kill another, or risk being shot in the back.

"We'd better get started, *segundo*," Sundance said.

"*Si, senor* boss," the old man said.

Chapter Two

There would be four Mexicans in the outfit and that was enough, Sundance decided after the old man left. More than four and they'd start calling it a Mex outfit. There would be trouble enough with the *gringos* without loading the crew with Mexicans. Sure, some of the big ranchers in Texas and New Mexico and Arizona had whole outfits made up of Mexicans. In fact, some big men liked vaqueros better than they did American cowhands, but that was different. When Mexicans worked for a man like John Chisum they stopped being Mexicans and became part of his ranch, his private cow kingdom. They were simply Chisum's men, just as the Southerners, Yankees, Germans and Irishmen were Chisum's men. Sundance knew that no such allowance would be made for him, so there had to be a balance in the outfit. To cut down trouble as much as possible was what he hoped to do. Trouble would come anyway; there was no sense asking for it.

It was well into the morning when he headed back for the American part of town. They were waiting for him. On the sidewalks men took their time getting out of his way, some wanting to dare him to take offense but lacking the nerve to do it. Small boys followed him in silence broken only by whispers and giggles. All he had in his favor was that he was ready to pay top wages. In hard times that might have been enough. Right now, in the early '80's, the cow business was booming and jobs weren't hard to find. Up in Kansas the meat buyers from the Chicago packing plants were taking away whole trainloads of Texas cattle, all they could find. There might come a time when the cow business fell into a slump, as most businesses did; so far it hadn't happened.

Sundance remembered the Alamo Saloon as a favorite haunt of jobless cowboys. Everything from beer to pig's feet and cabbage was priced lower at the Alamo than in the other places. A man could fill his belly without making too big a hole in his bankroll. The Alamo ran some whores, as did just about every saloon, but they were a dispirited bunch; down at heel and over the hill, aging women who had spread their legs times beyond number.

On this sun-bright April morning all the business in Brownsville seemed to be somewhere else. The Alamo had batwing doors tied back to save on wear and tear, and when Sundance went in, four men were at the bar, two at a table playing cards for nickels. A whore was going upstairs with a man so drunk she had to help him. Business was so slow that only one bartender was needed, washing glasses in a sink under the bar. The sink was in two sections and he washed in one and rinsed in the other before he set the glasses out to drain on a board with holes in it.

There were no Mexicans there and everybody stared at Sundance as he came in. The bartender knew who he was; they all did. Sundance ordered a beer and got it without an argument. Now and then he got an argument from bartenders who quoted him the law against selling alcohol to Indians. Sundance had a way of explaining that always got him what he wanted. This bartender didn't even try. He worked the handle of the beer pump, cut off the foam with a wooden paddle, and slid the mug across the bar.

The bartender didn't sound like a Texas man and maybe he didn't care one way or another about Sundance. Being a city man from up north, maybe he thought he was funny.

"Been in town long?" he asked.

Sundance guessed the bartender thought he was funny. After he asked the question he looked around for smiles of appreciation. He got a few guarded grins. They knew who Sundance was, knew a few things about him. Their tight grins said they knew he was a man with a hard reputation.

"Just got here," Sundance said. It went against the grain to be pleasant to the son of a bitch behind the bar. But he was in the cow business now and he needed a crew. At the Alamo, even more than in other bars, the bartender was the main source of information about the outfits that needed men, the ones that didn't. Sending men in the right direction put a few dollars in his pocket.

"Just got in," he repeated. "Is that a fact now. Looking for some kind of a job, are you?"

"Looking to offer jobs," Sundance said, sipping the beer. "I got a cow herd about ready to cross over from Mexico. I want to hire an outfit to drive them to Montana. You happen to know any men might be looking for work?"

The bartender began to polish the whiskey glasses; the beer mugs didn't rate that much attention. He must have been a refined barkeep, because he didn't blow his breath on the glasses to get a better shine. "Montana you say? Why not Kansas? Nobody ships beef from Montana. Where would it go?"

Sundance said, "It's not going anywhere."

"You mean you're trailing the herd up there for some rancher?"

Sundance remained patient. "The beef is going to feed the Cheyenne."

"An army contract?"

"My own contract, if you want to call it that. I'm still looking for men. What's the difference where the beef is going?"

That got a smile from the bartender. "There might be a difference. No offense, mister. Most people think the reservation Indians have it too soft as it is. Then there's another consideration. You're not buying Texas cows. People might say that's taking bread from American mouths."

Sundance finished his beer and got ready to talk directly to the men in the saloon. "Then you don't know any men?" he asked the bartender. He put a silver dollar on the bar. "I'll pay top wages. If a man gets sick or hurt he won't be left behind. If he's too bunged up to go on, I'll see that he gets home."

One of the drinkers spoke up without waiting for an answer from the bartender. A gangling man of not more than nineteen, kind of dumb looking, in range clothes dirtier than usual for a man not working. He had been sprinkling salt into his beer to give it taste. To Sundance he had the look of a binge drinker, one of those men who drank up their wages but could work well enough when there was no more whiskey left. There was nothing unusual in that; it was standard with most cowhands. So there had to be some important reason why he was out of a job in good times.

"I'm looking for work," he said, ignoring the bartender's warning frown. "The name is Charlie Starbright. I'll sign on if you'll take me."

The bartender cut in, not wanting the cowhand to work for Sundance. Or maybe he didn't want to lose his commission as a man who fixed up jobs for drifters. "I don't know that you ought to speak so fast," he said, watching Sundance. "You'll get a job one of these days. You have to wait for things to cool down. I told you I was working on finding you a place."

Starbright said, "It's been three months, Paddy. How long is a man supposed to go on paying? What happened was an accident. Could have happened to anybody."

Paddy, still watching Sundance, didn't agree. "It happened to you, ol' fella. It was an accident, sure, but you caused it. A lot of good fat beef got killed just a hundred miles shy of Dodge City."

"No men got killed."

"You caused Mr. Gannon to lose money. You know how he hates for that to happen. You're lucky he didn't hang you for it."

Charlie Starbright found no comfort in that. "I might as well be dead. I'm close to starving as it is." He gulped down the salted beer and made a face. "Have to drink this slop 'stead of decent whiskey."

"You're drinking it on credit," the bartender said. "You don't like it, try and get credit across the street. Do that but don't come back here."

The other drinkers were listening hard. "The hell with waiting," Starbright said, turning back to Sundance. "I know your name, mister. No use pretending I don't. You're Jim Sundance. You want to sign me on. I worked for Amos Gannon for three months. Before that, two years on the Brazos with Timothy Speer. Big Tim won't take me back because of what happened with Gannon."

Sundance moved down the bar and away from the other drinkers. Starbright took that as a sign to join him. The bartender named Paddy came along. "Set up a bottle and I'll take another beer," Sundance said.

"Sure thing," Paddy said. He came back with the drinks and Sundance told him to stick around. Paddy lowered his voice so the other drinkers couldn't hear. "If you're talking a little money I'll stick around. I got to be careful, see."

Sundance let Starbright pour his whiskey to see if he had a shake in his hands. His hands were steady but he needed the drink. He got a nod from Sundance and drank more whiskey and wiped his mouth with the back of a dirt stained hand. "That puts some steam in the boiler," he said.

"What happened with Gannon?" Sundance knew Amos Gannon by reputation. They said he was hard but fair. Sundance had heard more about the hardness than the fairness. Powerful men made their own rules, set their own wages, and decided what was fair.

"Made a stampede happen," said Starbright, getting the go ahead on another snort of liquor. "Aw, the whole blamed thing is foolish and I'm a fool. Damn me if I'm not. Old Gannon has this tomboy of a granddaughter he takes along on drives. You ever hear a thing like that? True, even so. Favors her above the other grandkids, swears she'll be running the whole spread some day. Foreman couldn't squawk and if you knew Gannon you'd know why. Kid traveled right along with the herd in her own wagon. Not a regular wagon though, more like the sheepherders' wagons you see up north. Wooden roof, oil sheet windows, regular built-in bunk fixed to the floor, small stove and pipe for the cold nights."

"Get to the point, Mr. Starbright," Sundance said. The bartender was grinning at the cowboy's story. The other drinkers didn't grin because they couldn't hear it. But they knew it too.

"Honey! That's what caused the stampede," Starbright said. "The cookie fixed special meals for this brat of a kid. Pancakes lashed with honey, she gobbled that up with half her meals. Most of her meals. So there was a whole box of honey jars for the little bitch."

"Charlie has a craving for sweets," the bartender said.

Starbright gave him a sour look, forgetting about the tab slate for his beer drinking. "Well, I do and I did. Drinking is forbid on Gannon drives, and he goes on all of them. Not that he has to. To look after this blasted she-child. Now when I can't have a drink I get a craving for sweet things. Honey's my strong favorite. Said I to myself, how's cookie going to miss just one jar outen a whole box?"

"Charlie fed honey to the cows and got them wild," the bartender said.

"Not a-tall," Starbright said for Sundance's benefit. "Herd was bedded down for the night.

Late and quiet, me in my blankets still awake after standing the second watch. Couldn't sleep thinking of that honey. Cookie'd kill me but he was snoring. I thought he was. So I snuck over to the chuckwagon and was opening the box of honey when cookie comes up quiet ahind me and grabs at me. I like to shit with fright! I got such a skeer I fell up agin all the pots and pans hanging there and brought the whole damn thing down, crashed it all down."

"Charlie spooked the whole herd," the bartender said. "Set them running wild, the suddenness of the noise. The whole outfit turned out to stop them. That right, Charlie?"

"You wasn't there, Paddy," Starbright complained. "I guess that's the way it happened, mister. In the dark they run for miles, then there was this cliff and the first wave of cows went over it like water. Fifty or sixty fat cows went over, got all broke up at the bottom, afore the rest of the outfit got them turned back from it. We didn't get the herd settled till full morning. Cookie blabbed to Gannon, afraid he'd catch it, them being his pots and pans. So, mister, I was for it. Gannon wanted to hang me, said he'd whip the hang horse himself."

"How'd you get out of that?" Sundance asked, knowing that Amos Gannon was the kind to do it. On the trail the owner was the only law. He could hang a man and make it stick. In a way, Sundance could understand Gannon's anger. Losing fifty or sixty good cows would make any man uncork his temper. Charlie Starbright was one dumb cowboy.

Starbright said, "They had a rope on my neck, was dragging me to a horse and looking around for a tree when this damn brat kid took up for me. Spare this poor man's life, Grampaw, begged the kid, I think enjoying herself. I don't know if Gannon was mad at me for killing cows or stealing the kid's honey. You're a fool, Charlie, a dangerous fool, Gannon says to me. I am heartsick and sorry, Mr. Gannon, says I. You got the money to pay for sixty cows? says Gannon. Course you don't, you dumb reckless fool. Look at that sweet little girl a-begging for your worthless life. The cows ran the other way, they could of killed my granddaughter. Only on account of her is why I don't hang you. I reckon I'll be drawing my time, sir."

"Charlie has nerve," the bartender said.

Sundance didn't agree. Charlie Starbright was a fool. "What did he do, whip you out of camp?"

"Lashed me with a rope end till I had stripes on my back," Starbright said. "Have some of the marks still. You think that was fair, Mr. Sundance?"

"I'll pass for fair," Sundance said.

Starbright had a drink. "All right, that part was fair. What he did later wasn't. Blackballed me in the whole cow business, is what Gannon done. Passed the word nobody was to hire me. I wasn't fit for nothing but swamping out saloons, sweeping for storekeepers. Maybe you don't want me either."

Sundance smiled. "If you don't start any more stampedes. Stay away from the chuckwagon between meals, Charlie. I guess you'll do."

Starbright had enough whiskey in him to display pride, half-hearted though it was. "I won't work for less wages 'cause Gannon put a black mark on me. No sir, I won't do that."

Sundance said, "You draw the same pay as the others. Now get your saddle and get on over to Mexico. The herd is outside town. Find the herd, then find my *segundo*, Francisco Aldama. Tell him I said you're hired. He'll find you a horse from the string. Don't give him any lip, Charlie. If you think Gannon is tough, just try back-talking Aldama."

"You mean I'll be taking orders from a Mex?" Charlie didn't like the idea. No Texas cowboy would.

"You'll take them and like it." Sundance showed Charlie the door. "Go or stay. I got to talk to Paddy here."

Starbright went out and Paddy said cagily, "You're asking me to get myself in trouble."

"Who'd make the trouble for you?"

Paddy watched the other drinkers without appearing to. That was a bartender's trick. "A funny thing, I don't rightly know. The word is out not to help you any way. I know there's feeling against the Indians. What's here is stronger than that. It's not like you were taking the beef to fatten the Comanches. They're Texas. You say you're gong to Montana. Looks like somebody big has a grudge against you. I hear there's money being passed out, not to help you."

"You get any of it?"

"I got some, not as much as I'd like. You want to match and double what I got? No use asking me who paid me. Some man, all I can tell you. Never saw him before. Spoke like me, from up north."

It was possible that Paddy was telling the truth about not knowing the stranger from up north. Sundance guessed he hadn't been given any fifty dollars. If the Ring had to start laying out cash, their agents in Brownsville wouldn't be throwing fifty to every man who might help them. But this was no time to haggle over a few dollars.

Sundance said, "Make it a hundred then. Half now, half when you find me some men. I know it can't be done in here."

"That's for sure. You got a place I can send what I find? You'll have to take what I can get."

"For a hundred you better not send me a lot of drunks and misfits. I'll take a drinker but not a drunk. No Mexicans, I got enough. Irishmen are all right, no wild brawlers." Sundance thought of the dangers ahead. "All right, brawlers if they're not too crazy. No railroad Irishmen. They don't know how to ride. What I need most is a cook."

"I'll have to search hard to find you that," Paddy said. "You'll be wanting another beer and I'll go get it." He left his drying towel on the bar. "Put the fifty under that. Do it when I get them looking at me."

Sundance waited while Paddy went to pump up his beer. While he was doing it he pretended to hurt his thumb, holding it up and cursing. Heads turned away from Sundance and he slid a fifty dollar Mexican gold piece under the bar-rag. Coming back with the beer, Paddy said in a loud voice, "You can drink beer all day, mister. You'll never raise an outfit in here. But that's your business."

Paddy slid the beer to Sundance and picked up the towel and stuffed it in his pants pocket. Now that he had the fifty, his manner became more hostile. "You've come to the wrong place," he said so all could hear.

Sundance drank some of the beer, left the rest.

"I'll be in the back room of the Benito Cafe, the Mexican quarter. The back door leads to an alley. Your people can come in that way."

"You'll have to trust my judgment."

Sundance smiled. "I trust you, Paddy. If you do wrong by me, I know your name and where to find you."

This time Paddy didn't have to take his scowl. "No need for tough talk. What about the other fifty?"

"The bartender at the Benito will have it."

"How do you know he won't steal it, say he never got it?"

"Because he'll be afraid of a very old Mexican with a fast gun. Mention the name Francisco Aldama. Get it right and you'll get your fifty. I'm in a hurry, Paddy. Get somebody to take your place if you have to."

"That'll cost you a day's wages. That's extra."

"Get the men and you'll get the money."

"Don't come back complaining if you don't like what I send."

Sundance turned to leave. "I'll do more than complain. How long you had this job?"

"Five years. Why?"

"Then you probably want to stay on in Brownsville. That won't be possible if you plant a spy on me. You do that and I'll find you. Texas is a big state but I'll find you. Believe the truth when you hear it, Paddy. Do your best and I'll pay you, even say thanks. But I mean it about the spy. Doubleshuffle me on this and I'll kill you. Now's the time to start telling me off. Don't go too far or they won't buy it."

Paddy had Sundance's money but he didn't like

him. He raised his voice, sounding more like a city guttersnipe than he had before. "Will you quit pestering me," he yelled. "Go on over to Mex country is my advice. You'll get no help from me, nor from any decent Texas man. There's the door. That way is OUT!"

"The hell with you!" Sundance cried. He was out the door.

Chapter Three

Now recognized as a good friend of the famous and fearless Don Francisco Aldama, Sundance was an honored guest at the Benito Cafe. No effort was spared to make him comfortable in the bare back room. The only thing on the card was roast goat, but the bartender, who was also the owner, assured him the *cabrito al hornito* had been prepared from freshly killed kid and was more tender than chicken. Maybe even more so. However, said the proprietor, if that did not suit his taste, they would prepare a steak such as he had never eaten in his life.

"Roast kid will be fine," Sundance said, realizing that he hadn't eaten since he left the train early that morning. "And plenty of coffee," he said. "Black and strong as you can make it. Bring a bottle of whiskey and glasses. Men will be coming to see me by the back door."

The proprietor said he understood perfectly. "If they come by the front door they will not be friends?"

Sundance had already checked the alley that ran behind the cantina. One side of it was open, and stringy chickens pecked and fought in a wire enclosure. Empty boxes and barrels from the cantina stood against the back wall of the building.

It was dark now and he would turn down the light before he opened the door to let the first man in. There was a chance that no one would come, at least not the men he expected to come. No, that was wrong. He didn't expect, he didn't hope. If they came it would save time. If others came it would be to kill him.

There was no window in the back room, a holdover from the days when all Brownsville had been Mexican and went by another name. The Mexicans were a practical people; a back room was for privacy, so why waste money on a window?

Sundance pulled the table away from the center of the room and over where a window might have been. Once there had been a stout heavy door; now it had dry rot in places and a shotgun blast fired from the alley would blow it down in a cloud of dust. For what it was worth it was barred and his callers would have to knock. The proprietor had been gracious, had barred the door for Sundance's safety. It was the wrong kind of safety, for to open the door he would have to stand in front of it to remove the bar from its slots. That was when a shotgun blast could come, if it came. Sundance lived by a few simple rules; two of them were: never take unnecessary chances and trust no one but the oldest of friends. Never standing in a lighted doorway was part of rule number one.

It had been more than a hour since he left the Alamo Saloon and went back to Greasersville, as the whites called the Mexican quarter. No one had come in that time and he would have been suspicious if they had. Paddy would have to move cautiously before he talked to men in a hostile town. At the moment he could be telling everything to the agents of the Ring. He wouldn't go back and kill Paddy if he betrayed him; he hadn't come so far to kill sneaky bartenders. And the journey had been hard, not the train ride from Washington, which had simply been dull. His journey, the one that brought him here, had begun many months before, whe he made up his mind to buy a good herd for the Cheyenne. For a long time all the reports about the condition of his mother's people had been bad. Worse than bad, they were starving. In Boston there were people who lived on nothing but greens, potatoes, fruit. He was pretty sure that such people had never lived through a winter on the high plains, eating nothing but greens and roots, wild onions and berries. In hard country people needed meat and the fat that came with the meat. It was as he had told Francisco Aldama: the meat they gave the Cheyenne was rancid or harbored disease. Or it was horse—or mule meat. Very old horses, very tough mules. That would change in five months. Anyway, that was the plan.

The proprietor came in with a steaming platter of roast goat, then went back to get the coffee and a cup. He brought the whiskey and stood waiting. A short, round-faced man in a candy-striped shirt and baggy cotton pants, he looked far from tough. Earlier in the day, behind the bar, he hadn't been wearing a gunbelt. Now he was. Much noise came from the cantina when he opened the door.

Sundance, pouring his first cup of black Mexican coffee, decided that here was a determined man if not exactly a tough one. The Mexican said casually, "If they come by the front door they will not get this far. A guarantee, *senor*, one you may rely on. From the street side you will be safe, as if guarded by a small army."

"Business good tonight, is it?" Sundance said. The coffee couldn't have been more to his liking. When he was away from Mexico he missed the goodness of Mexican coffee. He cut a slice of roast kid and tasted it, deciding that the kid had lived well past kidhood. He wasn't under oath so he nodded appreciatively.

The Mexican, smiling slightly, said business was usually slow, yet tonight there was a good crowd out front. "Of course, you understand, I invited a few friends. Friends of mine, Don Francisco's friends and, by your leave, friends of yours."

Sundance drank more of the scalding coffee. "Then all I have to watch is the back door?"

"Of that there is no doubt," the cantina owner said in Spanish. "You would have me invite a few friends to watch the alley?"

"No. They might be seen or heard. Some of my callers will be nervous and I wouldn't want to scare them off."

The Mexican bowed. "Don Francisco said you would know what to do." He waved away the money Sundance put on the table. "It is said that you fought with Juarez?"

"I had a small part in the fight," Sundance said.

The Mexican sighed apologetically. "I was in it too but on the other side. French officers and their Mexican puppets came to my village and invited every man under the age of fifty to join the army of Maximilian. It is hard to say no with a pistol at your head. I was a very bad soldier. I did manage to shoot a few officers in the back. A small effort, the best I could do."

Sundance poured another cup of coffee and let it

cool while he cut another piece of meat. "You know many of the *gringos* in Brownsville?"

The Mexican smiled. "You would have me look in now and then?"

Sundance pointed to the sliding panel set into the wall through which drinks could be served without opening the door. Below the panel was a flat board where bottles and glasses could be placed. "Leave that open a crack," Sundance said. "As you say, look in now and then. If you recognize a man who shouldn't be here, knock on the door and ask if I want more coffee. When I hear that I'll know I have to be careful."

"But suppose you want more coffee?" the Mexican said.

Sundance smiled. "This will hold me."

Nothing more could be done after the Mexican went out and closed the door. Sundance saw the serving slot go back about three inches, and he was just about through with the meal when the first knock came.

"It isn't locked," Sundance called out. The leather retaining loop was out from behind the hammer of his long-barreled .44. There was no need to move. He was set up as he wanted to be, chair against the wall, the table close enough to provide cover, plenty of room to draw and fire. He could get to the Colt as fast as if it lay on the table in front of him. It shouldn't be necessary to remind them of how dangerous he could be. All of Brownsville knew it by this time.

A man who might have been a gambler or a preacher came in and Sundance pointed to a chair. Whatever he was he wasn't doing too well at it. He had to be broke or he wouldn't be here, or he could be an agent of the Ring in threadbare disguise. Sundance decided that he was all right, as far as it went. The clothes could have been bought in one of the secondhand stores run by Chinamen or Syrians on the edge of Mex Town. But the desperate look in his eyes had to be the real thing.

"A drink first?" Sundance asked. Paddy's first choice didn't look too promising. Sundance reserved decision: what a man looked like now didn't tell what he might have been once upon a time.

A gambler, Sundance knew when the stranger reached for the bottle. Long hands, large hands, supple and quick. Hands that would dwarf a deck of cards. Hands that big and fast made it possible to deal cards any which way. Sundance guessed he'd been caught dealing off the bottom. Hence the shabby look of the gambler who couldn't find a game.

"Jules Bowdry is who I am." The stranger downed his drink and waited to see if the name meant anything to Sundance. It didn't.

"Mr. Bowdry." Sundance nodded. He didn't mention Paddy's name. "You know what you're here for? Could be our friend made a mistake."

"No mistake. Years ago I worked for Kenedy and Goodnight."

"Among other things. How many years ago?"

"Five," Bowdry said. "Make that ten."

"Five or ten, Mr. Bowdry?"

"Closer to twelve," Bowdry answered. "Twelve is the truth. You believe that?"

"How long doesn't matter, Mr. Bowdry. Doesn't matter if you can still do it. You want to tell me what brings you to this? A gambler looking for a cow job?"

"Money is what, the money I don't have. I'm strapped, Mr. Sundance."

"You got caught?"

"I got caught. I started out lucky but my luck turned sour. Ask me why and I can't tell you. People said I was the best. No brag, sir, I was the best. Gambling was forbidden in the Kenedy outfit. We did it anyway. Even as a kid I was good with my hands. Quick, what they call handy. When I was with Kenedy I made twice as much gambling as I did working. I got so good I knew I was in the wrong line of work. I kept thinking about quitting but I didn't have that much confidence. Kenedy made it easy for me, told his ramrod to run me off."

"You've been at it ever since?"

Bowdry turned the whiskey glass in his big, soft hands. "Till about a year ago. I guess I lost my nerve months before that. I'm telling you this. Why not! You'd be told."

"I'd ask," Sundance said, pushing the bottle forward with his left hand.

Bowdry wasn't so greedy with the second drink. He forced himself not to be. Sundance knew he wanted to gulp it. Bowdry didn't sound much like an ordinary cowpoke turned pasteboard mechanic.

"So you would," Bowdry said. "One night I felt my luck running out. A feeling I got. I couldn't shake it. All gamblers are superstitious, me as much as the rest. In the past I usually won, at least never lost so it mattered too much. That night, the one I'm talking about, I began to lose straight across the board. That was when I started to cheat. When you know how to cheat you don't need luck.

I don't know. I felt bad about it. It meant I wasn't so good any more. My hand worked fine while I was cheating. Not so when I tried to go back to playing straight. Every time I did that I started losing again."

"So you kept on cheating."

"Till I got caught." Bowdry's wintry smile was warmed for an instant with self-satisfaction. "It took them a long time to catch me. I'd won, usually I had, so nobody was surprised when I kept on winning. But all the time I was desperate. I knew they'd catch onto me, so I decided to go whole hog, make a killing and quit. Get into some other line of work."

Sundance poured coffee and it was no more than warm. He drank it anyway. So far a honey-craving fool and a broken down gambler. The gambler wasn't in yet.

"What stopped you?" Sundance asked, reminding himself that he couldn't be too picky. The herd was massed and ready to move. A lot could happen if he didn't get an outfit together.

"A big game, biggest I ever been in." Bowdry seemed to remember the game with some wonder. You're just sorry because you got caught, Sundance decided. You should have stuck to cheating farmers and travelers in ladies underwear. You'd still be gambling if you'd done that. "Biggest game held in San Antonio," Bowdry went on. "A-once-a-year game, they called it. A rich man's game. Big merchants, ranchers, an ex state senator, the richest undertaker in town. I knew the politician because I'd played with him a few times. I wasn't part of the group but the politician said I could sit in, only I'd have to put ten thousand on the table before I got to see a card. I just about made it, sold everything I had, got together every cent I had in the world."

"But you got caught."

"Took them a while to do it. Into the game I waltzed, well dressed, got introduced after I opened my wallet and tossed that ten thousand on the table like it was nothing. Over and above the ten thousand I had forty-two dollars. But they had no way of knowing that. I don't know. Maybe my fear had a smell to it. It was so jumpy I started drinking. I can drink and play. That night I drank too much. Guess I got careless when the game started to go against me. I knew the undertaker was cheating and maybe I looked at him too hard. It came my turn to deal and was dealing when the undertaker said in a loud voice, 'I believe you dealt that last card off the bottom, sir.' "

The gambler gulped his drink. "Maybe they'd been tipped off. I got grabbed from behind and had the deck taken away from me. Then they all started laughing like they were in on the joke. 'Why you're nothing but a lousy tinhorn, Mr. Bowdry,' the undertaker said."

Sundance said, "They knew the undertaker was cheating, doing it badly. He cheated so you'd get reckless when you began to lose."

Bowdry said yes. "You called it right. The men behind me held guns on me while these rich men decided what to do with me. They talked and laughed like I wasn't there. Hanging's too good for him, said the politician. How about jail, said one of the merchants. Some other man said I'd just corrupt the other prisoners. 'I'm old fashioned,' said the undertaker. 'Let's do it the old fashioned way.

Let's tar and feather the thieving son of a bitch. Run the sneaky bastard out of town on a rail. That's what they did. I don't know whose idea it was to give the story to the newspapers. That finished me. Not a man in Texas doesn't know my name. You want to hear what it is?"

Sundance said no. "What I want to know is can you still sit a horse? I don't mean just sit. Ride and rope and chase strays from dawn till dusk. Can you still shoot a gun, night guard a herd without nerving up the cattle?"

"They call me Featherhead Julie in the saloons," Bowdry said, as if he hadn't been listening.

Sundance said, "Can you do what I asked you? How old are you? Thirty-five? All right, you're thirty-five and you haven't done a man's work for twelve years. You're soft all over."

Jules Bowdry said, "I can get back in the swim. I need this chance, Mr. Sundance. Paddy said Montana. That's where I want to go. Maybe on to Canada after that. I'll work like a dog, you give me this chance."

It was a hard decision to make. "You bet your backside you'll work. Not like a dog, like a man. Twelve years at the gaming tables is poor training for that. I don't give a damn what you've done in the past. I'm not asking you to become a blood brother. Damn it—answer me straight. You think you're up to it? Think before you answer. You're wrong if you think you can bluff your way up into Kansas where maybe they won't know you in Dodge or Abilene. I find you're bluffing I'll turn you loose on the trail a hundred miles from nowhere. Try your card tricks on the hostiles, see how far that gets you."

Bowdry's lean face, pasty from a thousand all-night poker games, flamed a sickly red. He looks like an angry consumptive, Sundance thought. A lung case in a rage.

"Kick a man when he's down! You're no better than the rest!" Bowdry started to get up. He fished in his pocket and came up with two bits. "That'll have to do for the drinks." He threw the coin on the table and it rolled off and was lost in the thick sawdust.

"That's more like it," Sundance said. "Sit down and listen to me, Bowdry. If I had a choice I wouldn't pick you. You weren't in a spot, you wouldn't be begging a cowpoke job. Maybe that makes us even. You're hired if you still want the job. Yes or no, I don't have to repeat what I said."

Bowdry spotted his two bits shining in the sawdust and stooped to pick it up. Sundance saw the Mexican's eye at the slit in the serving door. The Mexican just looked and went away. Bowdry put the two bits in his vest pocket.

"I need to get to Montana," he said. "They know me in Dodge and Abilene. In Hays City and Wichita."

Sundance told him to go to Matamoros. "Look for a Mexican named Francisco Aldama." He peeled bills from a roll of greenbacks. "Buy some range clothes and a beltgun before you talk to him. You still got a deck of cards?"

"Like hell I do!"

"Buy a deck."

"What the hell for?"

"Card tricks," Sundance said. "You'll have five months to do card tricks."

Chapter Four

The next job seeker tried to kill Sundance and came close to doing it. It happened about twenty minutes after Jules Bowdry had stuffed the money in his pocket and left the way he came in. Sundance knew he was taking a chance on Bowdry. With money in his kick Bowdry seemed to brighten up and straighten up, and that could be a bad sign. The money to buy clothes, working boots and a pistol wasn't that much. But it would take him a fair distance if he decided to head north without benefit of company.

The man who came in after the knock had a New England twang that nothing could disguise, and he made no effort to do so. Wesley Perkins was his name, he said laconically but in the straightforward Yankee manner, originally from the Down East lumber town of Clear Lake Mountain. "That's the west part of the State of Maine," he said. "We got lumberjacks out that way make these Texas bravos looks like sissies. I hear you got jobs open for men that wants to work."

No sir, he allowed, sitting down, he didn't drink a drop but would smoke one of his own cigars. "Used to be quite a drinker when a lad," he said. "Hard cider, applejack, Canuck whiskey, anything I could throw my lip over. Was headed for a drunkard's death till I heard the Reverend Neal Dow—that's the temperance feller—speak in the town of Millinocket. I been a confirmed dry ever since. Now sir, about that job?"

"You're a long way from home," Sundance said. "Being a dry isn't all you have to be to get the job."

Perkins allowed himself a dry Yankee laugh. "What you mean is, what's a lumberman doing in cow country?"

"It's a thought, Mr. Perkins."

"So 'tis, Mr. Sundance." The Yankee puffed the small room full of rank tobacco smoke. "Well sir, I been a lot of things besides a timber beast. Was a drummer boy in the Civil War. First Maine Volunteers. Came through it and went home to work in the trees again. Didn't like the fierce winters anymore, so I lit out for warmer climates. Not much I haven't done since then."

Yankees were a gabby bunch no matter what the legend said. So were the so-called silent Indians. The only really silent people were the mountain folks of the Southern mountains. Perkins, for all his talk, didn't look too bad.

"We're talking cows, Mr. Perkins," Sundance reminded him before he began the recital of all the trades he had worked at.

"Done plenty of that too." The Yankee put more smoke in the air. "Was in Texas during Reconstruction. During the War my Maine outfit got to be part of the reg'lar army. Took a bullet in the knee outside of Austin. Reb bushwhacker, and mind you the War was a year over by then. Guess you noticed I limp a bit."

Sundance said yes. "It bother you much?"

"Hardly at all," Perkins said, squeezing his knee with his right hand. "Was in a military hospital and healed up fine but got discharged because of the knee. That made me mad. I figured to stay on in the military and become a general. In this man's army they don't give you money to get home. I got home in stages, didn't like it, came back to Texas. They hated Yanks back then, still do. They hated New England Yanks worst of all, claimed we started the war."

"You did," Sundance said. "You got a hate for Southerners, is that it?"

"Just Texans. I can't blame my knee on the whole South. Tell the truth, Mr. Sundance, for all how I sound I know the cow trade. Was ready to join an outfit when I heard talk about you. What you're trying to do is no secret, sir. Knowing I'm a Yank they warned me—some men, locals too—to have nothing to do with you. That got my back up. Maine people can be stubborn, you may have heard."

"You'll have to prove yourself," Sundance said. "Nothing against you, just business. I pay top wages and don't care if a man drinks or not, provided he does the work. I think you got a mean temper, Mr. Perkins. Never mind your knee, the War's over and there could be Southerners in the outfit."

"They don't bother me, I don't bother them," Perkins said. "The way you just talked, that mean I'm hired?"

"If you prove out when we start taking the herd across. I hope to start sometime tomorrow."

Perkins got his back up. "I wouldn't come here without something to show. I got a letter from Mr.

Ben Fiddler of Pedernales. Got it right with me."

Perkins' right hand dropped below the table and Sundance shot him out of his chair. He was a small, wiry man and the force of the bullet drove him back across the room. As he went over, a double-barreled derringer dropped from his left hand. He died without a word. Sundance was standing over him when the Mexican proprietor and three other Mexicans burst in with drawn guns. One of them had a .60 caliber musket cut down short and loaded with three or four lead slugs. The three Mexicans went out to check the alley while the proprietor remained with Sundance.

The Mexican kicked the dead man in the face. Then he crossed himself in the presence of violent death. "God rest his soul, the dog! He doesn't look like a killer."

Sundance knelt beside the body and went through the pockets. He found four fifty-dollar gold pieces, a woman's garter and a clasp knife. Nothing to say who he had been, the surest sign of the paid killer.

"You didn't expect him to walk in here like a gunslinger." Sundance kept the derringer but left the cheap knife. The derringer was a good one, definitely not the kind you could order through a mail order house in Chicago. For what it was, it was a finely made weapon, sturdy and heavy, a Remington rimfire with two three-inch barrels, one atop the other. A .41 caliber single action with a stud trigger. If you knew how to use it you could knock down a man at fifteen or twenty feet. Two .41 bullets fired under the table at such close range would have blown Sundance away.

"But how did you know?" The Mexican turned

the dead face with his toe. "I looked at him and knew I hadn't seen him before. He looked so open faced. It was different with that gambler you hired. I kept my pistol cocked and ready as I watched him."

"The gambler's no killer," Sundance said. "I don't know what else he is."

The Mexican scratched his head with the front sight of his pistol. "But how did you know?"

"At first, just a feeling. He was too open about everything, didn't have to drag a thing out of him. Told me more than I needed to know, in fact. Not always a bad sign."

"Then how?"

Sundance said, "I caught on that he was left-handed after a minute. Yet he kept using the right hand for everything. If he had been right-handed, like he made out, he would have kept his cigars in his lefthand shirt pocket. You see the other cigars are still in the right. Most men do it the regular way—they reach across."

The right-handed Mexican reached across to touch a pencil in his left pocket. He smiled with ferocity, appreciating Sundance's powers of detection. "He could have been different."

"True," Sundance said. "I wouldn't have shot him because of where he carried his cigars. He used his right hand too much, is all. You'd think his left hand was crippled, the way he kept it so still. He did everything right-handed so I'd be watching that hand. Then when his right hand dropped his left arm straightened out. That put a derringer in his left hand."

Sundance rolled up the dead man's coat sleeve. It was wider than the other sleeve but not so you'd notice it. Above the elbow the arm was encircled by a steel band lined on the inside with rubber. Attached to the band was a criss-crossed length of steel, something like the gadgets storekeepers use to take down cans from high shelves.

"A spring gun," Sundance said. "Move your elbow in a certain way and the spring puts a gun in your hand. Quicker than any draw when you learn how to use it. You have to practice a lot so the spring won't send down the gun at the wrong time. See the hinges? Lubricated with oil and graphite. Doesn't make a sound. Tricky but still a good idea."

The Mexican gaped. "A good idea! How can you say that?"

Sundance smiled as he used both hands to take the split steel band from the killer's arm. "A gift for you."

The Mexican had been looking at the spring rig with covetous eyes. "You don't want it? I have heard of a such a gun. Never have I seen one."

"Too tricky for me," Sundance said. "Like I said. If you move your elbow the wrong way you can find yourself with a gun in your hand at the wrong time. You may be talking to somebody you like but his natural response is to shoot you. Here, take it."

The Mexican regarded the spring gun as a gift beyond price. "I will have to buy a coat with loose sleeves." He shut the gate of the spring gun and put it in his pocket. "Loose sleeves and a derringer of the same size."

The three Mexicans came in from the alley and said everything was quiet. Mex Town was used to gunfire during the night hours. "If they were there, they're gone now," one of the Mexicans said in Spanish.

"My guess, he worked alone," Sundance said. A pool of blood was soaking into the sawdust on the floor. "The body?"

"It will be as if he never existed." The Mexican snapped his fingers and ordered his men to get rid of the trash—the Spanish word was *basura*—on the floor. "The Gulf is full of hungry sharks," he said. "Before you have digested your supper this thing will be bare bones. You wish more coffee?"

"Coffee and some fresh sawdust," Sundance said. "I still have a lot of men to talk with. I hope I do."

He knew he couldn't hurry it. It would take a while to round up a crew.

Paddy had done his work well, or at least he had tried. Sundance couldn't be sure that he hadn't sent Perkins. Probably not, for all through the night the job seekers came to the rear door and knocked and waited to be allowed in. Some he gave a drink and a dollar and sent away as hopelessly unsuitable. One middle-aged man, a veteran cowhand by the look of him, would have been fine except for the way he twitched. Liquor had wrecked more than his hand, it had addled his brain so badly that for him there was no way back. His speech was slurred and he kept forgetting things, said he'd been working steady for Clell Callahan, the big rancher, until a few months before. Sundance knew that Callahan had been dead for many years.

He turned down a spry old Chinaman who said he could cook nothing but Chinese. Sundance gave him a dollar but he passed up the drink. Sundance smiled after he shuffled out. The boys would declare war if they had to eat chop suey for breakfast, lunch and supper.

He hired a Swede who knew more about horses than he did English. A big brawny man, he said, "I get use to cows, you bet." In the country less than a year, he didn't know a thing about Indians or how the whites felt about them. He knew he was in Texas but hadn't heard of Montana. Sundance gave him money and sent him across the river.

The big Swede stuck out his hand. "You don't ask Lars Lindermann's name. I tell you. My name is Lars Lindermann." They shook hands.

Sundance figured the Swede would be all right. In halting English, the Swede explained that he had been a corporal in the Swedish cavalry before he went to sea, got drunk in Galveston and was left behind when his ship sailed. He had worked his way along the Gulf coast until he got to Brownsville. The sea made him seasick and he didn't want to go back to it.

About midnight Sundance hired two Irishman, brothers, who came together. They didn't have Irish surnames, but they were as Irish as Paddy's Pig. One was Conor Pendleton, his brother was Francis X. He insisted on including the X when he gave his name. "But you can call me Frank, Mr. Sundance." Conor said he went by the name of Con.

True Irishmen, the Pendleton brothers weren't bashful about helping themselves to the whiskey. In no time at all they had emptied the bottle. Both wore plug hats and had worked at many trades. They had come to Texas from Georgia to work on a branch railroad that never got built. But they had worked on ranches, Conor said. Sundance asked him a few questions and he answered them right.

After three drinks, Francis X. displayed a certain amount of Irish bellicosity. "Could be you don't want to hire us 'cause we're Irish. There's lots don't like the Irish. Would you be one of them, Mr. Sundance?"

He got on the bad side of them, at least temporarily, when he asked if either could cook. Con glowered. "Woman's work! What you're looking for, sir, is a bad-tempered old man in a dirty undershirt and no teeth. Lots of them cooks is queer as a three dollar bill."

"Just so long as he can cook, whatever he is," Sundance said.

The Pendleton brothers said amen to that. Sundance guessed that Con, the younger one, fancied himself as good looking. "Just as long as he don't get queer with me."

"We'll keep a tight rein on him," Sundance promised.

Toward one in the morning he rejected a Spaniard—a real Spaniard, not a Mexican—because he had worked with sheep in Wyoming. Some of the sheep stink still clung to him. "Sheeps, cows, what's the difference?" he said. "Nobody will hire me because I have work with sheeps. They spit and call me a dirty, stinking sheepherder. Paddy tell me you don't care about the sheeps."

Sundance said, "Paddy is right. Sheep don't bother me. I'd hire you if you knew anything about cattle. You said yourself you can't ride a horse. Sorry, there isn't time to teach you everything."

Angry, dark eyes narrowed, the Spaniard

spurned both dollar and drink. "Your cows stink!" he said.

Sundance got fresh coffee and waited. Hiring men wasn't much to his liking. For most of his life he had worked alone. Now and then he worked with old and trusted friends. Talking to too many strangers got under his skin. And so far no cook.

The next man he hired didn't need the job, and he hadn't worked on ranches, but he had been around them a lot. He wore range clothes with laced boots instead of the cowboy kind. He jingled money in his pants pocket and looked well-fed. Sundance wondered what his game was. He spoke with an Eastern accent.

"My name is Rodney Bennington," he said. "Perhaps you have seen my work in the illustrated magazines. *Harper's*, *The Atlantic Monthly*."

Sundance was able to link the name to drawings of Western life, and decided that Bennington would be a fine artist when he got over what Easterners called the Romance of the West.

"I want to be the best Western artist who ever lived. I didn't just sit in New York and draw pictures from my head as do so many of my colleagues, I came out West and learned to ride and shoot and rope. You can't just watch men do it, you have to know how to do it yourself. I was a crack shot at college, first on my pistol team. I won't be modest, Mr. Sundance. Everything I do, I do very well."

Sundance studied the dude. "You ever been on a trail drive?"

Bennington smiled ruefully. "That's the one thing I haven't done. Ranch owners, most of them, don't mind me working around their home spreads. I do drawings of them, make them look manly and heroic—men of destiny."

Sundance couldn't resist saying, "Too heroic, Mr. Bennington."

Bennington, smiling, said he knew that. "I have to get published. Later, after I'm established, I'll draw the West as it really is. Now about this trail drive. . ."

Sundance knew why Bennington had never been on a drive—they wouldn't take him.

Bennington said what Sundance was thinking. "I've offered to work my way without pay—and they still didn't want me. Too dangerous, they said. I'd be dead weight. No offense and so on. They want seasoned men."

"Can't blame them for that."

"My friend Paddy says you can't be so particular."

Sundance thought Bennington was a fine artist but wasn't sure he liked him. Maybe he thought everybody in the cow trade was dumb. Noble looking, but bonehead dumb.

"I can brand too." Bennington threw that in to put more weight on the scales.

"The herd's been branded. It has to be so the Customs men can make a count. They'll do that when the cows come across." It was the middle of the night and he was still short a hand and a cook. "If you come along you won't just give a hand when things gets tight. You'll work your ass off, Mr. Bennington. The drawing has to come second to the work. You'll have some free time, the work has to come first. You ever work a real cowhand's day? Up before first light, work till after dark."

"You think I'm not up to it?"

"Maybe I do. My point is, you don't have to be up to it. Why do you want to put yourself through hell?"

Some of Bennington's excitement communicated itself to Sundance. "Because I want to know what it's like. A trail drive is what the cow trade, as you call it, is all about. Without the drive all the months, all the years of work mean nothing. A drive is the guts of the thing. I want to plunge my hands in and get them dirty."

"Or bloody."

"Paddy said there might be danger. More than the usual, I mean. He wasn't very explicit. Can you be?"

"You could get shot. That explicit enough for you? And I'm not talking about ordinary rustlers or hostiles."

"By God sir!" Bennington said in his Eastern voice. "It gets better and better with the telling."

"Then I'll tell you the rest of it."

Sundance explained about the Indian Ring and the trouble expected to get from them. "Unless I'm wrong they won't just make a little trouble along the way. They'll find the worst men they can buy, maybe stir up the hostiles even more. Stir up Indians that aren't hostile now. Money and liquor is all it takes. And plenty of new repeating rifles."

"Capital!" Rodney Bennington said. "I'd still like to go along. I'd like to very much. I'm well-armed though I'm not wearing a gun. I'm very well-armed, sir."

"Stay armed," Sundance said. "After this I don't want to see you not wearing a gun."

"I'll make you immortal," Rodney Bennington said, studying Sundance in the bad light. "You have just the right face for it."

"Try it and I'll stake you out on an ant hill." Sundance smiled at the young man's eagerness. "Draw all you like when there's time to draw. Just leave me out of it."

Bennington stood up and they shook hands. "Call me Rod, I hate Rodney."

"I'll call you Bennington," Sundance said.

Sundance was tired when the Mexican came in to say it would soon be dawn. Plainly, the Mexican wanted to go to bed. Silver stubble glittered on his brown face and his eyes were red-rimmed from lack of sleep.

Sundance stood up and stretched. "Thanks for everything. You better send the men home and turn in. Guess we'll have to make do without a cook. Least for now we will. Maybe in the next town. . ."

The Mexican opened the door and turned down the lamp after he pulled its chain and blew it out. Rattling the chain, the Mexican didn't hear anything but Sundance's gun was out, the hammer back. Somebody was coming through the alley.

The Mexican drew his own gun and moved to one side. The footsteps stopped and a woman stood in the doorway. She peered inside, the gray morning light behind her. Her voice was low, husky and tough. Not unpleasant, just tough. She carried a stained carpetbag.

"What're you standing in the dark for?" she asked.

"Something we can do for you?" Sundance set down the hammer and holstered his gun. The Mexican, deeply suspicious, kept his gun in his hand.

"Not you for me, me for you," she said. "I hear you're looking for a cook. I can cook anything that walks or swims or flies. You need a cook and I need a job. Well, answer up fellas. You going to ask me in or do you usually talk business on the doorstep?"

"Step right in, lady," Sundance said, waving her toward a chair. "You had your breakfast yet?" He told the Mexican to start a fresh pot of coffee.

Going out to make it, the Mexican whispered, "I think you are making a terrible mistake, *senor*."

Chapter Five

"You are making a terrible mistake," Francisco Aldama repeated a few hours later. The old man was up in arms. Then, remembering his position as *segundo*, or lieutenant, he changed his tone to one of simple astonishment. "A woman on a trail drive brings bad luck. A woman cook is sure to bring disaster. You haven't slept in much more than a day. That's it, not enough sleep. Stretch out in the shade and sleep for a few hours. I'll wake you when the herd is ready to move. You'll feel differently after you get some rest."

Sundance looked at the herd massed about fifteen miles from the river. The cattle were well shed and in good flesh for such an early season of the year. Every cow there had been pased by Don Francisco himself. Only cows that looked as if they could make the long journey had been accepted. They were still on the Mexican side of the Rio: a thousand she-cattle three and four years old, two thousand five-year-old beeves. Fifty extra cattle of each class had been added to make up for losses on the trail, rounding out the number to thirty-one hundred. They had been raised at Don Francisco's ranch in the interior; all were in good, strong condition.

"Well, *senor* foreman?" the old man demanded.

"We'd be headed for a worse disaster if we

started without a cook," Sundance said. "We could manage a few days or so. Beyond that we'd find ourselves in trouble. It's not like we could drive three thousand cows up to a farmer's door and ask his woman, please lady, how about cooking a meal for us. Most likely we'd get shot at. You want that to happen?"

The herd was made up of long-legged, long-horned Mexican cattle, mostly pale-colored, which could run like deer, and at an ordinary walk could travel with a horse. Francisco Aldama's men were still there guarding the herd, waiting for Sundance's men to take over.

"But a woman!" the old man said. His rage got the better of him. "You have hired a WOMAN!"

"She sure looks like one," Sundance said. "And a mighty good-looker at that. What have you got against good-looking woman? I have heard many tales about you and beautiful women, in the days before you married your wife, of course."

Francisco Aldama didn't find that funny. "No one appreciates a good-looking woman more than I do. But not on a trail drive, *senor* foreman. If you had to invite bad luck, why couldn't she have been old and ugly and fat?"

"Maybe she'll gain weight," Sundance said.

"That is not AMUSING!" Francisco Aldama raged. "And this crew you hired! I have been a ranchero for fifty years and never yet have I seen such a crew! A tinhorn gambler! A thickheaded Swede! Not one but two ill-tempered Irishmen! A man who draws pictures! Where is the Eskimo? Where is the Chinaman?"

"I had the Chinaman but he couldn't cook American." Sundance smiled at the old man's sarcasm. "The Eskimo hasn't turned up yet. Old friend, you know I did the best I could. It's the woman that bothers you. I tell you there was no one else."

"I know and yet she bothers me. She will make for trouble far out on the trail. How can she not make trouble? I have seen her. I think she is the kind that enjoys making trouble. Those saucy eyes, that insolent mouth, the way she swing her hips."

"She claims to be a great cook. We'll know how good she is in a minute. Wonder what she's getting up for the noon meal?"

Francisco Aldama took a brandy flask from his hip pocket, unscrewed the top and used it as a glass. It was a short drink. "I don't care if she's the best cook in North America. What do you know about her?"

"No more than what she told me. Name's Molly Early and she wants to get to British Columbia where she has a sick sister."

"Not a sick father, an ailing aunt? Did she ask you for money so her beloved grandmother can have an operation for her hernia?" The old man snorted.

"Didn't ask for a dime," Sundance said. "She's from Canada—British Columbia—and wants to get back there. Has no money so cooking for a trail herd is the only way. Old friend, I don't give a damn why she wants to go to Montana as long as she cooks good."

"Montana is not British Columbia."

"It's close enough. Soon as she draws her wages at trail's end she'll have plenty of money to get the rest of the way. Don't be so goddamned suspicious."

"I have a suspicious nature. I have lived many years because of my suspicious nature. Get rid of her before it's too late."

Sundance turned to the old man. "I didn't know you could cook."

Francisco Aldama eyed him warily. "You know I can't cook."

"Then you'll have to eat my cooking."

"Never! On my mother's grave—never will I do such a thing!"

"Then it looks like we're stuck with her."

A second drink of brandy cheered the old man. "All right, she will have to do for now. For a while there will be towns after we leave Brownsville. I was stupid not to guess your intention."

The girl who called herself Molly Early was stooped beside the cookfire, working quickly and efficiently. She ignored the *vaqueros* and the men of Sundance's crew. Some of the *vaqueros* rolled their eyes and made shapes in the air behind her back. In the bright sunlight her long hair, tied in a bun, glistened like spun gold. She wasn't tall but shapely and strong. She had good hands, Sundance noticed.

"No," Sundance said. "I don't mean to ditch her. She made me give my word I wouldn't do that if she held up her end of the deal."

Francisco Aldama scoffed. "Did you ask for the lady's word, *senor* foreman?" he inquired with elaborate politeness.

"I don't ask the word of people I don't know."

"Perhaps you intend to ask something else of the lady?" Francisco was always formal in Spanish. Now his sarcasm made him more so.

Sundance liked the old man too much to go back

at him. "You're a dirty old Mexican."

Francisco Aldama appreciated the suggestion that he was still capable of straddling a pretty woman. The thought cheered him more than the brandy. "Bad luck or not, it is pleasant to see a pretty face among so many ugly ones. Why do men cooks have to be so ugly and so often like ugly women? I have heard it said that in *your* country men sometimes use the cook as a woman."

"Only on the very long drives," Sundance said.

For a moment the old man was worried again. "This will be the longest drive of all and the cook is a real woman."

"No one is going to use this woman."

"Not even you."

"Not even me."

"Even if she came to you in the night."

"That would be different."

"The men wouldn't like it."

"There will be lots of things they don't like. So they won't get too excited we'll lay over outside Ogalalla and Dodge. The women there will have to hold them for the rest of the journey."

Turning from the fire, Molly Early called out. "Soup's on!"

That was just an expression. What the girl dished up was beef stew, good and thick with plenty of meat. She had pan-browned the beef chunks before putting them in the pot to simmer. The stew had potatoes and onions and carrots, flour for thickening. Unused to having a woman cook for them, the *vaqueros* and Sundance's crew looked at their plates with some mistrust. All but Rodney Bennington who said the stew was as good or better than anything he'd eaten in his life.

"More like goulash, don't you think?" he asked Sundance.

"It's good stew," Sundance said.

"Goulash is Irish stew with a Hungarian accent."

"I know what it is, Bennington. Eat it while you can. We won't be killing any beef on the trail."

Sundance saw that the young artist had taken a shine to the girl who called herself Molly Early. He ate fast so he could get finished before the others. Then he got out his sketch book and began to make a charcoal drawing of her.

She was dishing up her own lunch when she caught him at it and bristled. "What the hell do you think you're doing?"

Bennington was glib—too glib. "Sketching you in all your loveliness. You don't mind that, do you?"

Molly Early put her plate down and held out her hand. Bennington was a fast worker and the sketch was nearly done. "I do mind," Molly Early said. "I don't want you making likenesses of me now or later. Tear it up or give it here."

Bennington thought he had a way with the ladies. "Don't be so bashful. It's done and I think well done. I'd like to keep it."

Molly turned to Sundance. "Make him tear it up. I don't want it and I don't want him to have it."

Sundance nodded. He thought she was making too much out of a simple drawing. Still, Bennington hadn't asked her permission.

"Give her the sketch," he told Bennington.

"I don't understand why she's so upset."

"You don't have to. Give her the sketch—now!"

Furrow browed, Bennington tore the page from the pad and handed it to the girl. She glanced at it before she crumpled it into a ball and threw it in the fire.

"Tell him to keep away from me," Molly Early told Sundance. "He comes near me, I'll scald him."

Bennington was no more than five feet away. "I think he hears you," Sundance said. "Too much talk here. Finish up—we're taking the herd across."

All but three of Francisco Aldama's *vaqueros* had left and they were on their own. Sundance watched the experienced Mexican cowboys turn their horses south, and was truly sorry to see them go. The day was bright and clear, with an east wind that meant a flood tide in the river. The three remaining *vaqueros* were worth their weight in gold as they began to move the cattle to the ford known as Paso Ganado. The Rio Grande was two hundred yards wide at this point. The east wind brought a flood tide but the current wasn't too bad. The three *vaqueros* were sent ahead to the river to put the cattle in. On the Mexican side there was a single string of high brush fence on the lower side of the ford. It started well out in the water and ran back about two hundred yards, making a half chute by means of which the cattle could be forced to cross. The ford had been in use for years in crossing cattle.

"Bennington!" Sundance called and the artist

rode up close to him on his own pinto.

"Yo!" Benningtn answered cavalry fashion, touching his finger to the new style cavalry hat he wore, wide brimmed with the front turned up. Since crossing over to Mexico he had changed his shirt for a double-breasted dark-blue fireman's shirt and heavy wool pants held up by broad canvas suspenders. Atop the pretty pinto he looked like one of his own magazine illustrations.

Sundance said, "Don't stare at that bald hill standing up above the trees on the American side. You can look now. That hill bothers me. We'll be starting to cross over in a few minutes. That hill is a good place to shoot from."

Bennington didn't look in the direction of the hill. With the fringe of trees surroundings its bald top, it looked like the top of an old man's head. "I know what it looks like," he said. "I made a drawing of it this morning while we were waiting for you to get here. Even got a name for it—Dan'l Webster Peak."

Sundance glanced at the Winchester box magazine five-shot sporting rifle in its scabbard under the artist's right leg. It was the first lever action of its kind, with the highest velocity of any lever action available. It hadn't caught on yet and probably never would because the box magazine made it slightly clumsy and it cost considerably more than side-loading repeaters. Sundance had seen it tested, knew what it could do. With a velocity of 2400 feet per second, the five-shooter could penetrate fifty-eight pine boards 3/4 of an inch thick. Its caliber was .30 Army.

"You good with the boxer?" Sundance asked.

"Very good," Bennington said with his

characteristic lack of modesty.

"If there is somebody on that hill they won't start shooting till we start to bring the herd across. Tide isn't strong but it's starting to go out. If they can stampede the herd a lot of cows will be heading out to sea."

Bennington's right hand strayed to the stock of the new repeater. "Why not wait till the tide is at its ebb?"

"It would take too long. I want to get started now. We can't hang back every time there might be danger. You got field glasses?" Sundance hadn't seen any amongst the Easterner's gear.

"In my pocket. Smallest strong glasses they make—the best! I have a rich father, Sundance."

"Then don't get killed. The magazines wouldn't be the same without you. Now cross over like you're heading for Brownsville. Ride on till they can't see you from the knob. Then leave your horse and come back on foot. See what you can see. If there's a man in hiding with a long gun—kill him! You ready to go that far in your study of the Wild West?"

Bennington, dude or not, didn't even flinch. "Wait and see. How much time do I have?"

"Make it thirty minutes. If nothing happens we'll start bringing the herd across."

He watched as Bennington rode the pinto down to the swollen river and walked, then swam his pinto across. Nothing showed itself on the bald hill. He called Francisco Aldama. "Your *vaqueros* will take the cows into the water and head them straight across. We'll cut out three hundred at a time. You keep the Irishmen and Bowdry. I'll cross over with the Swede. Think you can hold the herd steady with that many men?"

Both men turned to watch Molly Early saddling a grulla, one of the horses in the string. She turned the handsome horse and got up close. "You'll need all the help you can get. Where do you want to put me?"

"Stay with the herd," Sundance said. "You know what you're doing?"

Temper flared in her clear green eyes; unusual eyes to see in a woman with yellow hair. "What the hell do you think?"

The girl and the old man rode back toward the herd. Ten minutes were left from the thirty he had given Bennington. Maybe there was nothing on the hill.

The Swede, mounted on a sturdy coyote pony, proved to be an expert rider. "Three hundred at a time, take it slow," Sundance said. "They're thirsty so there won't be any trouble getting them to the river. The *vaqueros* will steer then across. You know horses and they're dumb enough. Cows are twice as dumb. See that big beeve over there? I'll start with him and the others will follow the leader."

The Swede smiled at the quick lesson in cow lore. "Not so hard," he said.

"Sometimes it is," Sundance said, snapping open his dead father's English hunter watch, a bulky silver timepiece that never lost a minute. Five minutes to go, once they cut out the first batch of cows.

Francisco, the Pendleton brothers and Molly Early had to hold the rest of the herd now bawling for water. The herd moved restlessly as the first three hundred moved down toward the river. If the herd broke loose and ran for water at one time they were going to lose plenty of cows.

"Start this batch running," Sundance told the Swede. "The *vaqueros* will take care of the rest." The cows reached the water with Sundance and the Swede crowding them from behind. The three *vaqueros* were in the water, riding outside the fence to keep the cattle from turning when they reached the point where they had to swim. A rifle cracked from the hill, lifting the hat from Sundance's head. Then right after the first shot came the sharper sound of Bennington's sporting rifle. Two shots—that was all!

"Keep them moving," Sundance said, taking no heed of the hill. The *vaqueros* forced the three hundred cows into midstream and started them swimming. Sundance and the Swede got across faster than the cows. Then from the top of the hill Sundance heard a yell. Bennington was on the crest, jabbing the sky with his rifle. Sundance waved back. He made a downward motion with his hand, telling Bennington to take cover, to cover the rest of the crossing. The dude was all right, he decided.

Bowdry and one of the vaqueros, the thin, silent one named Jesus, stayed on the far side with the first batch, letting them drink in the shallows before moving them to higher ground. A long shallow sandy hollow went back for hundreds of yards, a natural holding pen for a good part of the herd. By the time the last six hundred cows came across, the front of the herd would be moving. Up on the hill there was no sign of Bennington.

Each trip across was the same as the last. One beeve, wilder or dumber than the rest, took a notion to swim out to sea. One of the *vaqueros*, Cesar, fetched him back. It was April but the water in the river was cold. As the herd on the American side grew larger, Sundance took the girl and one of the Irishmen and sent them across. It was Conor, the one who considered himself handsome. Going across he tried to pay down a line of blarney but the girl ignored him.

In just over two hours the whole herd was across and so were the men. "Head them out," Sundance told Francisco. "I got to see what Bennington shot."

"Maybe he just wounded the assassin," Francisco said in Spanish.

Sundance turned his horse away from the herd. "If he's wounded he won't be for long."

"Kill him a little for me if he is," the fierce old Mexican said.

Sundance dismounted and climbed up through the stunted pines that ringed the top of the hill. Before he got there Bennington stood up, smiling with satisfaction, pointing with the muzzle of the box-loader. Beside an outstretched right hand was a Winchester "take down" repeater with a round barrel. Most of his skull had been blown away by the high velocity shell from Bennington's rifle. The skull above the forehead was a mess of shattered bone and brains, but the face hadn't been touched. It was loose and sagging like a rubber mask that had slipped off. Sundance knelt beside the body and firmed up the face with his fingers. Bennington stared in horrified fascination, not looking as tough as he wanted to.

Firming up the face wasn't all that hard; the body was beginning to stiffen in first rigor. The eyes were closed and Sundance opened them; they stared open. He firmed up the chin and pinched the cheeks in.

"What in blazes are you doing?" Bennington blurted out when Sundance closed the dead mouth and turned up the corners in a ghastly grin.

Sundance stood up. "Say hello to Smiley McGuire. I thought it looked kind of like him. Lucky you shot from below or you might have wrecked the face. Or did you aim at his back and get him in the head?"

Bennington didn't like to have his markmanship questioned. Anger put some color back in his face. "I hit what I aim at."

Sundance picked up the dead bushwhacker's rifle and emptied extra shells from his pocket. "Next time aim for the middle of the back. It's not a fancy target but it's bigger."

Bennington, first man in his shooting team at college, resented the lesson. "I killed him with one shot, didn't I!"

"You did fine," Sundance said. "I'm glad you didn't tear off the face with that boxer. If you did we'd never know what we're going to be up against. It's going to be as bad as it can get. Smiley can't talk but he doesn't have to."

"You know him for sure?"

"For sure," Sundance answered. "Smiley there was a good shooter but never worked by himself. Didn't have the brains to think for himself. But a good shot, few better. If my horse hadn't stepped in a hole just as he fired I'd be floating dead in the river. You didn't just kill any old bushwhacker, Bennington. You blew away one of Larch Macdonald's top men."

Bennington started down the hill in front of Sundance. "Is that supposed to scare me? I never even heard of this Larch Macdonald and I've been all over the West."

"You'll get to know Larch as we go along," Sundance said.

Chapter Six

The men from the United States Customs were late, but Sundance knew better than to move the cows before they were counted. And maybe that's what the Customs men were banking on: that he'd move the herd, thus breaking the federal law. That would mean the whole herd could be impounded and he himself arrested for smuggling. Like the Lord, the Indian Ring moved in mysterious ways. Not just mysterious but downright sneaky.

They got there in their own sweet time but they got there. Sundance guessed they had been there all the time, watching from afar. If they hadn't come he would have telegraphed General Crook in Washington. Three Stars—Crook's Indian name, derived from the three stars of his rank—had been posted temporarily to the War College to lecture a class of foreign generals on the hard-hitting, irregular tactics he had developed during his Indian campaigns. Sundance knew Three Stars hated the job but it was good to know where he was.

One Customs man counted and the other, the fat one, supervised. Washington always used two men where one would have done the job just as well. The one who counted used a tally string tied to the pommel of his saddle, on which there were ten knots, keeping count by slipping a knot on each even hundred cows. The cows bawled impatiently but there was no hurrying the office holder with the soft job. Francisco Aldama counted in his own way, with ten shiny pebbles, shifting a pebble from one hand to the other on the hundreds. It was going to take some time.

The *vaqueros*, Starbright and the others kept the herd under tight control so the Customs men couldn't accuse Sundance of trying to sneak a few dozen extra cows into the brush that grew on both sides of the hollow. Molly Early was checking over the supplies in the chuckwagon.

Sundance figured Bennington had earned the time to get over killing his first man. The dude was taking it well enough.

"It'll stay with you for a while," Sundance said without taking his eyes from the counting.

Bennington was cleaning the five-shot but Sundance knew his mind was far away. "I wasn't thinking about him," he said. "This Larch Macdonald. You talked as if you knew him."

They were about halfway through the count. "Came close to killing him. You haven't heard of him, he's been out of the country for years. A Canadian. Years back a band of renegade Cheyenne ran to Canada with the cavalry hot behind them. The Cheyenne should have behaved themselves when they were safe across the border. The Canadians don't kill the Indians like down here. They murdered Macdonald's wife and kids—raped the wife, killed and scalped everybody. That day Macdonald was fifteen miles away teaching school."

"A schoolteacher!"

"Farmer and schoolteacher. Took turns. Taught school three days a week, farmed the rest. That night he came home to find his place still smoking, his family dead."

"The Cheyenne got away, is that it?" Bennington slid the five-shot into its scabbard.

Sundance said, "They didn't get away. Canada has good law, not like here. The Mounties took out after them and brought them in. It couldn't be proved which ones did the actual murders so they got life in prison instead of the gallows. Straight life, no time off, no parole. I guess they're still in there."

"That wasn't enough for Macdonald?"

"It wouldn't be good enough for me either." Sundance remembered how he had tracked down the drifters, white and Indian, who had killed his mother and father. He hadn't just killed them: they died in prolonged agony.

Bennington said, "I don't know what I'd do."

Sundance said, "Be glad you'll never have to decide. Macdonald decided to kill all the Cheyenne he could find, and not just the Cheyenne—any Indian he could find. First he started by himself, hiding out from the Mounties, killing and scalping peaceful Indians. Women and children, no difference. Fearing an uprising, the Mounties hunted him night and day. Macdonald was like a ghost, always got away. He built a reputation he didn't want. Indian haters, American and Canadian, outlaws passing as such, began to join him. Then the Canadians called out militia volunteers to help the Mounties. Macdonald and his gang skipped out of Canada and began raiding Indian villages in Wyoming and Montana. Then he started robbing banks as a sideline, or the hard cases talked him into it. More and more outlaws began to ride with him. He was killing reservation Indians so that made it army business. I was a scout then, with Crook. One night we set up an ambush in a Cheyenne village. Macdonald would kill any Indian but his real hate was for the Cheyenne."

"Hard to blame him," Bennington said.

"Not blaming," Sundance said. "Crook told me to catch him or kill him. I knew what he looked like from a picture the Mounties sent. They wanted us to send him back if we caught him. They came late at night and we wiped out half the gang. I wounded him but he clung to his saddle horn and got away. I tracked him three days. By then he was by himself but his horse had a cracked shoe and I tracked him by that."

"That shouldn't have been too hard to track." Bennington was still sore at Sundance for telling him how to shoot.

"Not hard at all," Sundance said. "I would have caught on that his horse was riderless except that Macdonald put a dead man aboard. Either he died of wounds or Macdonald shot him. He roped him over the saddle so the tracks looked right. I wasted days tracking the wandering horse. By the time I found the horse Macdonald had made his way to the railroad. I think he went eastbound, then got off, dropped off at some slow place so the conductor would have no memory of it. I figure he traveled back west and headed down to Mexico."

"I never heard a word about him," Bennington said.

"Didn't last more than a few months, the whole thing. Macdonald isn't a gunslinger, but he's a dead shot with a rifle. Made no legend for himself, so the story was over before it started. All this was over ten years ago. I doubt there are ten people know what he looks like."

"He got to Mexico. You know that for a fact?"

"For a fact. For two years he worked with the *rurales* and the regular cavalry in their campaigns against the Yaquis. Maybe he knew Spanish or learned it. I know he read Latin. That was in the description we got from the Mounties."

"A Latin-reading killer."

Sundance shrugged. "Quantrill read Latin and Greek. I served with him until he became more bandit than irregular. I lost track of Macdonald after the *rurales* wiped out most of the Yaquis, made slaves of the rest. Macdonald came out of that with bloody hands. What happened after that I don't know."

Bennington kept his voice steady. "The man I killed, Smiley McGuire. You have no proof he was still working with Macdonald."

"No proof but it figures. McGuire was Macdonald's wife's brother. He joined Macdonald soon as he could find him. Dumb as a heifer but a crack shot like his brother-in-law. Hunters as well as farmers. I think the Ring sent somebody to Mexico to get Macdonald back to the States."

"He wouldn't come just for the money."

"Private reasons don't count. The Ring will pay him well. But you're right. Macdonald will do anything to keep this herd from reaching the Cheyenne. It's been ten years and he never murdered anybody white. The law won't be looking too hard to bring him in."

"What about the army?"

"Phil Sheridan is commander in chief these

days. His solution to the Indian problem, so called, is to kill every man, woman and child."

Bennington stated General Sheridan's infamous words: "The only good Indian is a dead Indian."

Sundance said that summed up Sheridan's attitude. "Unless Macdonald starts killing Indians again, the army won't show much interest in him. If all he does is just attack a civilian trail herd the army will ignore him. I didn't tell you all of it. That herd belongs to me, paid for with my own money. So it's no government contract to supply beef to the reservation. We're on our own and what law there is won't be much help."

Bennington said quickly, "They're having a row over there." The artist was not a tall man and he had to hurry to keep up with Sundance as he strode over to see what the trouble was. When he got there the Customs man, the counter, was red in the face.

"What's the hold up?" Sundance asked, covering Francisco Aldama's right hand with his own. The old man's hand was resting on the butt of his revolver. Sundance squeezed the old man's hand and he took it away from the gun.

Francisco said, "This *cretino* says we are thirty cows over the agreed limit." He spoke in Spanish. "He cannot count or he is a thief."

"What's he calling me?" The Customs man appealed to his superior.

The head Customs man addressed himself to Sundance. "You're thirty head over. You'll have to pay duty on thirty cows. My man's been counting for years and never makes a mistake."

"Especially when it lines his pockets," Francisco Aldama raged.

The first Customs man forgot to get mad. "I thought you didn't speak American."

The old man drew himself up haughtily. "The language is also known as English and I speak it better than you do. Sundance, they are trying to gouge you for thirty cows you don't have. I counted before we left my ranch. We lost no stock on the way. I have just finished counting. Exactly the same, thirty-one hundred cows."

The Customs supervisor was a smooth talker and not at all bothered by the old man's anger. "I have to take the word of my own man. However, if you doubt the accuracy of his figure, then we'll have to do it again."

Sundance wanted to pull the supervisor out of the saddle and kick his fat ass all the way back to Brownsville. He knew the second count would be slower, delaying them for about two hours. This wasn't the time to argue with authority.

"How much do I have to pay?" He knew how much. He named the figure and there was nothing the supervisor could do to contradict him.

"You're entitled to another count."

Sundance knew the money would never find its way into the United States Treasury. "We'll let it go," he said, taking out the roll of greenbacks. It was getting thinner all the time. "Don't forget the receipt."

"Write him a receipt, Tom," the supervisor said, and would have said more but didn't have the guts. "A pleasant journey. Tell Montana Brownsville says hello."

His way of saying he hopes we don't make it, Sundance thought.

Not so many hours of daylight were left, but Sundance told Francisco Aldama to start the herd. With men on both sides, the herd strung out for a quarter of a mile, they began to move. Two riders, Starbright and Bowdry—the point men—rode out well behind the lead cattle, directing the course of the herd. The main body of the herd trailed along behind the leaders like an army in loose marching order, guarded by swing men, the three *vaqueros* and Con Pendleton, who rode out well from the advancing column to ward off range cattle and to see that none of the advancing herd wandered off or dropped out.

The herd was fat and well watered and inclined to behave, and when a herd is like that there is no driving to be done. The cows moved of their own free will. That was the true secret of handling a big herd, Sundance thought. Never let the cows know they are under restraint. Let the cattle do everything voluntarily, but from the moment you get them off bed-ground in the morning until they are bedded down at night, never let a cow take a step except toward the place you're going. If you did it right, you could just drift along, or appear to, covering fifteen or twenty miles a day. To move at that pace was harder on the men than on the cows: a good cowman's job was to make the difficult look easy.

Molly Early and her chuckwagon traveled to one side of the herd so vehicle and driver wouldn't catch all that dust. Sundance wanted to see how the girl handled the wagon. She could cook, but could she handle a wagon like a man? It was immediately obvious that she could, and not only that—she had secured everything that would make too much noise. Sundance thought of the stampede that Starbright had caused by his craving for honey. That was a fluke, a freak accident; at night all the cooking utensils would be out in preparation for breakfast.

Molly's wagon creaked and banged out but no more so than any chuckwagon on the move. If anything, she had gone beyond the usual limits of caution, wrapping the pots, skillets and tin plates in lengths of burlap. She had checked the stout ropes holding the water barrels in place, then added rope of her own. She handled the mules just fine, taking no nonsense from them. Sundance smiled: Molly, whoever she was, was a nononsense woman in matters of cooking and driving. There was a hint of wildness in the private side of her.

They left Brownsville behind and were glad to do it. Fort Brown was nearby so there wouldn't be too much trouble for a while. The army didn't concern itself with ordinary lawbreakers; still, the very presence of the military kept the wild ones in line. At least it made them cautious, for there were a few officers who bypassed their orders and shot badmen wherever they found them. Too bad there weren't more commanders in the same frame of mind.

The first and second day out there was no incident of importance. Starbright rode point as if he hadn't been a day out of a job. Bowdry sweated a lot and looked tired but knew what he was doing. For all his years at the gaming tables, he was shaping up pretty good. They made fair time and the *vaqueros* didn't have to be told a thing. They were Mexicans, and superstitious about many things but not about women. They liked having the girl along, and were almost gay as they worked. Francisco Aldama said they were the best men who ever worked for him, and Sundance didn't have to take his word. All mounted on their own blacks, they rode gracefully and without effort. The two Irishmen weren't half as graceful, and Frank Pendleton could be clumsy. But both knew something about trailing cattle, though not as much as they said. Accustomed to big cavalry mounts, the Swede was working hard to get used to the cow pony he was on.

On the third morning Sundance rode in advance of the herd to look for a crossing on the Arroyo Colorado, a sluggish bayou about forty miles north of Brownsville. Fifty feet wide between bluff banks, it wasn't as easy to cross as it looked. After a while Sundance found a place that didn't look too bad and went back to bring up the herd.

Sundance knew the wagon would have trouble crossing, and even the horses. In all there were twelve mounts in the string. So far Sundance hadn't said anything to Bennington about the pinto. Kids and ladies liked the look of pinto ponies—they were so pretty. Pretty or not, the pinto was not a good mount for hard work. This freak-colored animal was the result of in-breeding, and if you didn't work it too hard it was all right. But the pinto was dumber than any other horse, and not nearly as strong.

Sundance had kept the herd near the coastline for the sake of open country, but the sandy, sometimes marshy ground was something of a drawback. At times they could hear the murmurings of the Gulf on the other side of the sand hills and dunes. On the far side of the dunes was Laguna Madre, and beyond that the long straggle of Padre Island. Sundance decided that the herd would have to ford around the mouth of the bayou. A shallow bar had formed where the fresh and salt water let in the laguna. It was a lot wider here, almost two miles wide, but there wasn't more than a foot of water and the herd could cross nearly as fast as on dry ground. The day was drawing to a close and the herd was started at once. This was a good place to go across, because it was flat on both sides—no cover for snipers.

Once the herd was far out in the shallow water the wagon followed, and the horses came next. There was good footing on the sandbar, but the water was too salty for the cattle, though the loose horses lay down and wallowed in it before they were driven on. It took less than an hour to get the herd across, and when they got to the far shore the cattle were thirsty from their attempts to drink the sea water. Charlie Starbright knew the country north of Brownsville and said there was a fresh-water lake a few miles inland. They got there and bedded down the herd for the night.

Sundance knew he had to talk straight to the men. They knew that Bennington had killed a bushwhacker; more than that had not been explained to them. The *vaqueros* and Charlie Starbright didn't care. Constant danger was a fact of life in northern Mexico and Starbright was just glad to be working again. In spite of Amos Gannon, the rangy young cowhand would redeem himself in the eyes of other ranchers if he came through this drive in one piece.

The Swede shrugged and Molly Early said she

didn't give a damn about any Larch Macdonald. "I'll scald him too if he tries anything with me." It looked like Molly was ready to scald any man who approached her uninvited. Sundance wondered what it would take to get invited. It was a casual thought, for he had no intention of going near her. He wouldn't kick her out of his blankets if she came in the night; that would be plain foolish. But he wasn't going to pursue her. As the old man said, that would bother the rest of the men—and why get them muttering their resentment? Sundance hadn't asked the girl if she could shoot; such questions weren't asked of cooks. Most cooks kept out of the way of flying lead. If she had a gun she wasn't wearing it. Maybe it was in the carpeting she had stowed away in the chuckwagon.

Only Bowdry, the ex-gambler, showed some signs of nervousness when Sundance explained what they could expect from Macdonald. Instead of eating his supper he picked at it, not what you would expect a man to do after a long day in the saddle. But Sundance didn't fault him for being jittery; a man could fear death very much and still do his job.

"You ought to think about hiring a few more men," Bowdry said. He drank one cup of coffee after another and smoked a lot. "A suggestion is all I'm making."

After just a few days on the trail they were eating good. Supper was ham and beans, gallons of coffee. "I take it as a suggestion," Sundance said. "Have to watch the bankroll. But you're right. I was fixing to look for one or two extra hands."

They left it at that.

It was a good place to camp, with wood, water

and grass in abundance. Some range stock came nosing around and they chased them off. They watered the herd when they reached the lake and then a second time before bedding them down for the night. If not for the threat of Macdonald it would have been pleasant beside the big lake, with a campfire of dry oak logs blazing in the darkness.

Sundance put Cesar, Starbright and the Swede on the first watch. Jesus, Frank Pendleton and Bowdry were picked for the second. The third and last watch would be made up of the old man, Ramon and the other Irishman. Sundance wanted to keep the Irish brothers from standing watch at the same time. They were given to gabbiness and a night-bedded herd was used to humming or singing.

Molly was at the chuckwagon and supper was over but she could hear him picking the men. She reached into her carpeting, which she had stowed in the locked medical supply box, and took out a five-shot stubby Webley revolver, a .455 in the British caliber which also loaded regular American forty-fives. It was a good gun, Sundance knew, and could be loaded faster than a Colt because there was a hinge and a latch and the chamber and barrel swung down for loading.

"What time do I stand guard?" she asked.

Sundance liked the way she handled the heavy Webley. "You don't have to stand watch—you're the cook."

That angered her. "I'm a lot more than a cook. You know I can ride. Just don't ask me to guard with that artist. Where is he anyway?"

"Looking around out there. That was his idea. He'll be on the last watch. Cows always get a bit edgy before first light. If you have a mind to, you can join the first watch. I don't want a sleepy cook."

Anger made her tell him more than she intended to. "I haven't been a cook all my life." She caught herself and didn't reveal anything else. "All right, the first watch."

"Suit yourself." She didn't have a rifle, just the revolver from the bag, and Sundance told her to pick one that suited her best. He watched while she chose a fairly new '73 Winchester from the extra rifles wrapped in waterproof cloth in the wagon. She handled it as expertly as she did the revolver.

Sundance smiled. "That was good supper tonight."

"Hah!" she said irritably. "If that means where did I learn to cook, the answer is none of your business." She joined the men on the first watch.

Bennington gave the right holler so they wouldn't open fire on him when he came in from the dark. Hunkering by the fire, he poured coffee from the blackened pot still bubbling there. "If they're out there I didn't hear them."

"You wouldn't," Sundance said, drinking coffee himself. "Macdonald has been stalking men for too long. If he can stalk Indians without being heard, he sure as hell can stalk us."

Bennington said, "You make him sound supernatural."

"The Cheyenne began to think so when we failed to kill him. He's single-minded, that's all. Killing Indians is his life's work and he can't do that if he's dead. Killing him will be far more easy."

"This time you mean to do it?"

"This time I'll get more chances. I hope I will. A fact: we'll never get to Montana if we don't kill him. Macdonald is a strong leader with one bad flaw. A fatal one, I hope. He surrounds himself with tough men with thick heads. A few smart ones drift into his outfit from time to time. When they start to think for themselves they get killed. That's Macdonald's flaw, not keeping some of the smart ones. If he gets badly wounded there's nobody to take over till he can ride again. If he gets killed the whole gang will fall apart like baked mud. Kill Macdonald and we're home free."

Bennington was ready to get some sleep. "I've been thinking," he said. "And maybe you have too. That Early girl sounds like British Columbia all right. I've been there and know how they sound. More English than the rest of Canada."

"You have a point, Bennington?"

"You said Macdonald was a Canadian. You think there's some tie-in between them?"

It was possible, Sundance thought. It was like Macdonald to plant a spy in the outfit. He would have to keep a close eye on her. To Bennington he said, "You don't like her because she tore up your pretty picture."

Chapter Seven

Moving on, they kept to the coast, taking the herd away from it only when forced inland by the fingers of the Laguna Madre. A week out from the Arroyo Colorado they came to the Great Salt Lagoon, and had to drive the herd fifty miles in from the sea. This was their last sight of salt water, and the murmur of the Gulf died away behind them. It was warmer after they moved away from the dunes and sand hills and the stunted, wind-twisted trees that faced the sea.

Northward, the trail led through two of the biggest ranches in Texas, outfits that sent their own huge herds to the railroads in Kansas. The two ranches were so big that it took a week to cross them. They were watched by men who made no effort to hide, but this was open range and no attempt was made to stop them. So far there was no shortage of water for the herd. The Mexican cows were becoming well trail-broken by now, and for range cows they were docile and easy to handle. In order to keep them docile, water and good grass were all-important, and made for a quiet bedding-down at night. A fed and watered cow was a peaceful cow, wanting only to rest when darkness fell. Stampedes usually happened when cows were dry and hungry.

The *vaqueros* kept to themselves but the other

men began to talk, however guardedly, which was good, for when there was too much suspicion and hostility the cows would catch wind of it. Only Molly kept completely aloof, and while there were some complaints about this—mostly from Frank Pendleton—no one could find fault with her work. One day, hoping to get on the good side of her, Bennington picked a bunch of flowers for her. His reward was to have them thrown in his face.

Days later they reached the Nueces River and followed it for many miles because of the water, leaving it only where it made a sharp turn, doubling back to the southwest. After that for days the Atascosa, a tributary of the Nueces, became their main source of water. The herd remained well-behaved, moving north at a steady rate, giving no more than the usual minor trouble.

Then late one night they showed how fast they could run, how mean they could be. It happened during the second guard, in the darkest hour of the night, but it wasn't until first light that Sundance knew the stampede was no freak accident.

As foreman, Sundance didn't stand a regular watch. Tireless, he slept when he needed sleep, checking on all the watches between-times. The herd was bedded down on the north bank of the river, so there was nothing to hold them. Sundance had checked on the first watch and was getting an hour's sleep when he heard a yell that could only mean trouble. Along with the yell he heard the mad bawling of several cows. The man yelling was Charlie Starbright who knew all the signs of a stampede about to happen. So did Sundance.

The whole herd seemed to rise from sleep at the same time, and took off like jack rabbits, running as only pale Mexican cows can run. If the chuckwagon hadn't been standing behind a jumble of rocks it would have been kicked to pieces and the girl stomped underfoot. When the herd got to the rocks it divided and roared around them on both sides like an angry sea. Vaulting onto Eagle's back without a saddle, Sundance caught up with the running herd, trusting Francisco to give orders to the other men. The herd was running fast but Eagle caught up easily. The herd was running with too broad a front and could break up into two or three sections at any moment, and if that happened it could take days to round it up. They would lose plenty of cows if the herd split three ways.

Sundance had to circle out far before he was running with the herd and trying to get ahead of it. Riding without saddles, the old man's *vaqueros* and Charlie Starbright were closing in on the herd from both sides. Dust boiled up in the darkness, blotting out what little there was. The cows in front were still bawling crazily. A gap began to widen in the middle of the herd and Sundance knew it was going to split. Riding in as close as they dared, the *vaqueros* shot off their guns and yelled like banshees. Still the gap widened.

Sundance touched Eagle's flanks with moccasined feet and the great horse surged forward at the unspoken command. The only chance was to get in front of the herd and give the crazed cows something to follow, while the rest of the crew forced them together. Running wasn't a natural gait with cows, and if they could be kept together they would begin to tire before long. But they had to be kept on a straight course. Now, at last, Sundance was ahead of the running herd.

What he was going to do couldn't be more dangerous, yet he had to do it. He turned Eagle to the left and galloped straight out in front of the maddened cows. As long as the ground remained level and broken he was safe enough. But all it would take to bring him down was a gopher hole, a patch of rocks—anything! Horse and rider would be trampled to death; by the time the herd ran over them there wouldn't be much left to bury. On both sides of the herd pistols cracked and flashed in the darkness. Sundance dared a look, and the herd seemed to be coming together, stretching out long instead of splitting. Eagle jumped over something—a rock—and galloped on. Sundance rode in silence, and in the darkness he was a shape, a sound, something for the lead cows to follow. With Eagle under him he could have ridden far ahead of the herd. They would lose sight and sound of him if he had. He had to remain where the real danger was, a few hundred feet ahead of the running herd.

He rode a mile and most of another before all but the frenzied cows in the lead began to tire. The rest of the herd had run itself out and finally slowed down, milling around, bawling confusion. The lead cows ran on and Sundance made no effort to turn them. No more than ten or twelve cows crashed on ahead of him. Sundance turned and galloped back. The cows still bawled but they were through running for the night.

Now it was first light and the herd had been quiet for hours. The run had made them hungry and they bawled for water, tongues blackened by their own dust. As the sun came up, Sundance saw the thick spread of mesquite less than a quarter of a mile ahead; it wasn't just a thicket but a long, wide stretch that covered many acres of ground.

"Jumping Jesus!" Charlie Starbright said. "The whole herd would have been ripped to bits in there. You'd have lost half the herd 'stead of the handful you did."

Sundance and Starbright and the old man rode to look at the dead cows lying in the tangled thorns of the mesquite. Sundance got down and so did the others. Ten cows lay twisted and torn, flies already settling in the wounds, ants in columns in the mouths and ears and dripping backsides.

Starbright stopped beside a dead cow. "Look at the tongue all swole up. I'd say jimson weed but we're too far south for jimson."

"Not if somebody brought it," Sundance said.

"The salt around the muzzles," the old man said, touching his finger to the saliva that still dripped from the dead cow's mouth. He sniffed at the blob of saliva on his finger; even blackened by dust it had a yellowish color.

"Jimson," he said.

Sundance nodded. He didn't have to take the old Mexican's word. All the signs were there—unmistakable! "Macdonald figured where we'd bed the herd and got there ahead of us. Brought a lot of cut jimson and mixed it in the grass. Soaked it in salt so they'd eat it up."

"That's what he did," Francisco Aldama agreed. "Cows won't drink sea water because of the other things in it. Cows go crazy for salt."

"And jimson," Sundance said, thinking that Macdonald must have cut the rank smelling weed pretty fine before spreading it in the tall grass of the bed ground. It had been years since he'd heard of that trick, and he hadn't thought of it because Macdonald had been in Mexico, where jimson didn't grow.

Francisco Aldama mourned the loss of the fat cow as if it still belonged to him. "A good thing he didn't spread more of the loco weed."

"He didn't plan to poison the whole herd, just stampede it into the mesquite. He was afraid we'd catch on if he spread too much."

Charlie Starbright got back on his horse. "What's to stop him from doing it again, Sundance?"

"He knows we'll search for it from here on. That'll be part of your job, Charlie. Don't go looking for any of the flowers—you won't find any. My guess, you won't find it again, not unless it's growing natural."

When they got back to camp they found the rest of the crew cutting out range cattle that had been mixed into the herd during the run. This was slow work but it had to be done right. If they moved on with just one wrong cow they might find a posse coming after them. After the strange cattle had been cut out, they stretched out the herd in a line to make a count; except for the dead cows in the mesquite, it came out right.

Breakfast was eaten late that morning; Molly cooked with the Webley stuck in her pants pocket. The brown walnut handle stuck out, giving her a reckless look, like a lady outlaw. Maybe that's what she was, Sundance thought. To be sure, she hadn't led a sheltered life. She dished up coffee and a stack of flapjacks and ate as heartily as the men, taking no part in the talk about the stampede. She had been up all night, not that it showed in her face. She looked less tired than any of them. Before she started breakfast she checked the contents of her carpetbag, shielding it with her body while she rummaged through it. Only when she was satisfied that nothing was missing did she set on the coffee pot and the skillet.

Thinking of the dry country ahead, Sundance told the old man to take the herd back to the river but not by the way they had come. That meant a delay, but the cows were bawling with thirst. Tired or not, they might start running again if they didn't get water in the next hour.

On the move again, there was no regular trail to follow. It was all open country here and they moved as much as possible in a straight line. In a few days spring came to stay, and the prairie was carpeted with flowers. The jimson weed didn't grow here but Charlie Starbright rode ahead of the herd, beyond the point man, always on the lookout for other poisonous plants: monkshood and milkvetch. On the fourth day after leaving the river, he found a thick patch of milkvetch and they had to move the herd around it. The purple flower wasn't as dangerous as Jimson—nothing was—but the cow that grazed on it got mighty sick.

Water grew scarcer and they had to search hard to water the herd at least once a day. They passed to the west of San Antonio and kept well away from it because word would have gotten there from Brownsville.

On the far side of San Antonio was a real cattle trail, fifty or sixty yards wide in places, where all the local trails blended into one common trail known as the Old Western Trail. Millions of cattle had gone up this trail before them; it was as well defined as the course of a river.

A few times a day there were spring showers that helped the grass grow and the flowers bloom, but for all the rain, water became scarcer. The herd was restless again because three thousand cows could drain a prairie pond in no time. Sundance sent Charlie Starbright to scout for water well in advance of the herd. After two days he came back with bad news.

"We're in for a dry drive," he said with downcast eyes, as if he expected to be blamed. Charlie came late for supper and Molly made a quick meal, and there was plenty of coffee. Although he was nineteen Charlie wasn't able to raise much in the way of whiskers. Now he scratched at what he had. "We'll come to a small string of lakes, past which there is no water for about sixty miles. Feller I met said the country after that is bony dry."

Bennington had been sketching by firelight. Without looking up from his book, he said, "Other herds get through."

Charlie bristled, tired though he was after the long hard ride. "Begging your pardon, *Mister* Bennington, what this feller said was, sometimes there's water and sometimes there ain't. It could be we'll get there when there ain't."

Having put the artist in his palce, Charlie spoke to Sundance. "A lot of cow tracks heading west this side of the lakes. We could do the same: go west along the lakes, then I'll scout north some more."

Sundance said no. "Westbound tracks don't mean there's no water directly north. They could mean ranchers taking cows west, and nothing more. We can't spare the time to head west."

Charlie grew sullen. "We face drought if you're wrong."

"You forget your place, young man," Francisco Aldama said coldly, no doubt wondering why Sundance didn't jump all over Charlie. "We go where the boss tells us to go."

Before Charlie could talk back, Sundance told him to get some sleep.

In the morning they started out again and it took four long days to reach the lakes. Charlie said the lakes were called The String of Pearls, and there were seven in all, natural reservoirs with rocky bottoms, about a mile apart. The water in them was clear and cold, fed by underground springs. The cows smelled water from a long way off and bawled madly in their hurry to get there. Along the lakes there was good grazing for cattle and horses. They approached under a setting sun and by the time the cows were watered and bedded down it was dark.

Believing that soap and water removed essential oils from the skin, the *vaqueros* refrained from bathing. So did the Pendleton brothers though they, along with the ex-gambler, washed weeks of trail dust from their faces. Only Sundance and Bennington braved the water, bone-chattering cold. Bennington yelled when he dived in and when he came to the surface Sundance told him to shut up.

"Well looky there now!" Bennington said in an imitation of a Western song. "Our lady of the reeds!"

Molly Early was naked and washing herself in the shallows, partly screened from view by the tall reeds that grew along the shore. After she scrubbed vigorously she wrapped herself in an unseamed flour sack and went back behind the chuck wagon to get dressed.

"Wouldn't I like to stew her apples," Bennington said, unwilling to leave the chill water before Sundance did.

Sundance, chest high in cold water, ducked under to scoop up a handful of clean white sand. He scrubbed his skin until it tingled. "You've got a bigger horn than any cow in the herd," he said.

Bennington laughed. "Not in water this cold I don't. All my desire is in my head."

"Keep it there," Sundance said. "That woman is capable of putting poison in your food."

After the bath and before supper they changed the water in the chuckwagon barrel. Then they washed out and refilled the extra twenty-gallon keg. They posted a strong guard during the night, but nothing happened. In the morning, after the herd had been watered again, they moved on, hating to see the last of all that good water.

Soon they were out in semi-arid country and the horses had to work harder than the men to control the herd. Changes of horses were made all through the day so as not to exhaust any one horse. In the string of horses, or *remuda*, were sorrels, grays, coyotes, a brown, and a *grulla*. After watching Bennington, working hard as anyone, Sundance ordered him to find a better mount than the pinto.

"I trained the pinto myself," Bennington argued.

Sundance didn't have time to argue. "I didn't say you had to shoot him and maybe we'll need him yet. You taught him to prance and he keeps on doing it. That's a dumb horse, Bennington—too slow and tires too fast."

The artist did what he was told but it didn't make them any better friends.

Water got so scarce that the herd had to be allowed to lie down and rest several times a day. They lost time every time they had to do that. There was no help for it. Thirst made the cows restless and the point men had to ride steadily in the lead to hold the herd to a walk. There was good grass but without water the herd didn't graze very much, only when the heat of the day was over.

Nearly four days were used up getting the herd forty miles from the string of lakes. Then Sundance rested the herd for a whole day and said they would move by night. Molly and the chuckwagon, with the Swede as an escort, went ahead about twenty miles to make camp on the near side of a long ridge. It was after dark when they got there. When the campfire blazed like a beacon, Sundance ordered the herd to move on. The moon came out, washing the prairie in yellow light, and there was a cool breeze. All the days were hotter now.

It took most of the night for the herd, moving slowly, to graze its way to camp. The campfire was there to give the cows a sense of direction. A few hours remained before dawn and the cows were bedded down to rest.

Prairie gave way to tableland and there was hardly enough water for the men. They used it sparingly, but after breakfast on the third day out from the lakes there was hardly enough to fill their canteens. The coffee pot no longer bubbled on the fire and they drank the juice of canned tomatoes and peaches. Nobody complained except the Pendleton brothers, both complainers by nature.

The next day was as hot as if it was midsummer instead of spring; the tongues of the cattle hung out and they bawled in a kind of rage. No more rain could be expected for a long time, and as the ground dried out the dust got worse. The breeze died and the dust hung in the still, hot air, motionless and eye-searing. The men rode with their bandannas over their mouths and worked frantically to hold the herd to a walk.

By afternoon Francisco Aldama reported that there wasn't enough water for the horses. A horse gave out faster than a cow because all a cow had to do was walk. On top of the old man's bad news, Molly had bad news of her own. A few inches of water sloshed in the bottom of the extra keg, and that was the end of it. An hour later they came to a waterless creek that wasn't completely dry after they dug a deep well in the center of the bed. It took a long time for the well to half fill with muddy water that tasted as bad as it looked. They let the horses have it and soon it was dry: even the wet mud had been licked up by the thirsty mounts.

That night there was no sleep for anyone, and it took all their efforts to keep the herd from running. Sundance wasn't sure they would be able to hold the herd till morning, and the sky said the next day was going to be a sizzler.

The sun came up and there wasn't a breath of air, not a cloud to soften the hard blue sky. Two hours out on the trail the heat was almost unbearable and the cows were feverish and close to panic. Crazed by heat and thirst, the lead cows began to turn back and to wander aimlessly. The cows from the rear pushed ahead and the herd began to lose shape and direction. Crowded together, the cows got hotter and thirstier, and some lay down and had to be goaded to their feet. It took hours and a lot of yelling and the firing of six-shooters to get the herd back in some kind of shape, but when the shock of the noise wore off, the herd drifted again, formless and rebellious, bumping against the horses and men that sought to bring some sort of control.

Francisco Aldama, gray with dust, spurred his horse close to Sundance. "The signs are the worst," he said.

"Yes," Sundance agreed. "The herd is going blind."

And he thought, Macdonald doesn't have to do a thing. The whole herd will die soon if we don't find water.

Chapter Eight

There was no way to turn back and try to find another trail to the north. Past the point of no return, they had to go on. The next day was worse than the one before, and by now the cows that weren't ready to run themselves to death began to lie down; some never got up again. Soon the men began to suffer as much as the cows as they crawled on under the pitiless blue sky. Hardest hit of all, the horses began to falter, and even the chuckwagon mules, hardiest of animals, began to bray their discontent. Through cracked, brownish lips the two Pendleton brothers complained constantly of their hard luck in joining such an outfit, instead of waiting in Brownsville for a railroad job. Sundance didn't give a damn how much they ran off at the mouth, as long as they kept it to themselves, but by the third really bad day they were talking openly to the other men, mainly to the Swede and the ex-gambler.

The sun was a huge brass ball in the sky when Sundance turned his horse and rode back to where the Irishmen were. They were talking hard to Bowdry and he was listening with a glum look on his face. Earlier they had been working on the Swede, filling his thick head with their stories of death by thirst. They shut up when Sundance came near.

Frank Pendleton did the thinking for his brother and he greeted Sundance's order to break up the prayer meeting with sullen silence. There was no mutiny yet, but it might come.

"You move over to the left," Sundance ordered, pointing at Frank with his left hand, keeping his right hand free to kill if he had to. Both Irishmen wore pistols on cartridge belts paid for with his money, and he'd be damned if he let them throw down on him.

"What difference does it make?" Frank said. "This whole herd is coming apart. We got no more control over it. One more day like this and we're done for."

Sundance said, "You want to quit?"

Frank had no ready answer but he wanted to argue. "We should have gone west along the lakes. That made sense but you said no. Now look where we are."

Sundance asked him again. "You want to quit? How about you, Bowdry? You been listening to all this talk?"

The ex-gambler didn't have the nerve to look directly at Sundance. But he said, "Looks like we're going to die out here."

"You were starving to death when I picked you up in Brownsville," Sundance said. "You want to go back there"—he pointed—"it's that way. You made a contract with me, so I could take your guns and drive you with a whip. You too, Pendleton."

Dull hate showed in Frank's red-rimmed eyes. "You won't drive me with a whip. You'll have to kill me before you do that."

"Then I'd do that. Think you can outdraw me, Frank? You and your brother can try it. I'll blow your gunhands to bits before you can get off a shot. Then I'll hang you. No trees out here so you'll hang by dragging."

Bowdry, sick-faced, kicked his tired horse and got out of the way. "I want no part of this," he said. "They're the ones was talking."

"Find somebody else to talk with." Sundance hadn't taken his eyes off the Pendletons while the herd drifted aimlessly ahead, moaning for water. "Go on back to Brownsville, Frank. Take your brother with you."

Con Pendleton said, "We could make it back to the lakes. He's letting us go, Frank."

Frank was smarter than Con and he knew what Sundance intended to do if they decided to go. Frank said, "But not like we came, is that it?"

Sundance heard Francisco Aldama riding close to him. The old man reined in his horse but didn't say anything.

"You'll have to walk, Frank." Sundance waited a moment. "You don't get a horse. Nothing here belongs to you. You don't get water and you don't get to keep the guns. Another thing: before you leave, peel off your clothes, boots, hats. Everything belongs to the outfit. Make up your mind, the herd is moving."

"That would be the same as killing us," Con blustered.

His brother told him to shut up. Frank Pendleton wanted to go for his gun—it was in his eyes—but his hand stayed where it was. "Son of a bitch! Either way we die, that's what you're saying."

"I'm saying you'll take any order I give you. You don't have to like it—just do it! I could hang you for mutiny and leave you for the coyotes. If you stay on, keep your mouth shut and do your work. There won't be a second warning, Frank. I'll kill you where you stand."

The old man spoke for the first time. "I think I would like to hang that one. The *lengua larga,* the long tongue. I have had to do that more than once. I know his kind. He will listen to the warning but you will have to watch him all the time."

Sundance didn't want to kill anyone except Larch Macdonald. "I'll watch him," he said. "If the warning doesn't work, there are quicker ways. You take charge of them, Don Francisco."

The old man smiled a weary smile. "You are very formal today, Senor Sundance."

"Killing is a very formal business," Sundance said.

Thirty cows died of thirst before they found water on the fifth day. It happened after the herd had rested all night. No one had slept for two nights. Molly rode herd because there was no water to cook with and the canned goods had run out. They bedded the cows in a waterless valley with sloping walls, the only place where there was any hope of controlling the crazed animals. An hour before sun-up Sundance sent Charlie Starbright on ahead in the dark to search the country for water. Sundance expected him to be gone four hours, even half the morning, but he rode back waving excitedly while the sun was just coming up. Sundance half pulled him out of the saddle before the commotion he made caused the cows to get more restless than they were. As it was, the speed of his arrival and his babbling voice brought a good part of the herd to its feet.

Sundance clapped his hand over Charlie's mouth and shook him into silence. "You found water?"

Remembering the first stampede, Charlie whispered more than he had to. "A big prairie pond just a few miles ahead. Cows didn't smell water 'cause the winds coming from the north."

"How big a pond?" Sundance knew that the young cowhand had a way of exaggerating things, and a little water might be worse than none. If the first cows to reach it emptied the water, the rest of the herd would go wild.

"Big enough to hold us," Charlie whispered. "Enough to get us to the Concho."

Sundance let Charlie go and told Francisco Aldama to get the herd ready to move. "How do you think they'll take it?" he asked, meaning the cows. "It can go two ways when they get close enough to smell it."

The old man shrugged. "They are half dead and half blind. Who knows what they will do. If they run wild all we can do is save as many as we can. Maybe we should move them there in batches of two or three hundred."

"No," Sundance said. "We'll move them at the same time. The ones left behind might go crazy. Give Molly and Charlie a thirty minute start so they can fill up on water. No use watering the herd if the rest of us go dry."

Sundance found Molly and told her to hitch up the chuckwagon and head out. Charlie helped her with the harness. "Take everything you can fill, every canteen," Sundance said. "Then take the wagon well away from the pond. I mean, far away. If a stampede starts I don't want you buried under it."

"Don't worry about me," Molly said.

"I wasn't," Sundance said, smiling at her quick temper. "I just don't want to lose that wagon."

Francisco Aldama sprung open the cover of his large gold watch and stood waiting. The other men, their nerves about played out, waited too.

The chuckwagon was well out of sight when the wind changed and the cattle got their first smell of water. A quiver ran from one end of the herd to the other, but nothing else happened. The herd began to move of its own accord, but slowly, and as the old man said, the cattle were ready to lie down and die. The pond was only about two miles away, but it took the herd the best part of an hour to get there. When they did get there, finally, they did something that only Sundance and Francisco had ever seen before—they walked into the wide pond almost indifferently and stood there silently, no longer bawling, rib deep in the water, drinking very little.

Francisco said, "If cows can think, that's what they are doing. They are trying to remember what water feels and tastes like. Now watch them come out and rest in the grass along the edge of the pond."

And that's what they did. In batches or singly, the cows moved out of the pond and some stood for a while before bedding down to rest. Only a few stayed in the water, and it was only when the sun was up in full force that the whole herd, still behaving well, went back into the water to drink their fill. Then they rested and drank throughout the entire day. There was no way to hurry them on, and no need.

Watching from a faraway hill, Molly drove the chuckwagon back and set on pots of coffee after Charlie helped her with the fire. Ordinarily, she would have told Charlie to go look after his cows, but on this blazing hot morning she was quiet and very tired. The men came to the chuckwagon to get their canteens and she was civil, if not friendly. Only once did she snap at anyone, and that was when Bennington, in his sometimes irritating way, asked if she would dip her finger in his coffee to make it sweeter.

"Sugar's all used up," the artist said.

Molly didn't return his smile. "Too bad you're not gone." She turned away to scrape the last of the sourdough from its barrel. It was beginning to smell bad in the heat, after weeks of travel, and when Sundance came to get coffee she said it was time to start thinking about supplies.

"The next town or settlement we come to," Sundance said.

"Better make that soon," Molly said.

Well grassed and watered and back to their normal contrariness, the cattle moved on with almost no trouble. Molly was right about the supplies: they were down to weak coffee and flapjacks fried in bad-smelling lard. By now they had been on the trail for most of a month and the first day of May found the herd just over five hundred miles from where it started. During the last week in April they had moved the herd across the immense tableland that skirts the arid portion of west Texas. They pased Blue Mountain, the first upthrust of the hills that mark the headwaters of the Concho River. They found more water on the way, and in the deep grassed country, the herd began to fatten up again, getting its strength back and regaining all the valuable beef that had been lost in the days of drought. The only setback on this part of the journey was a stretch of rocky country which some of the cows got lame and sore-footed crossing.

They reached the Concho; so close to its source it was narrow and easy to cross. Up till now they had suffered the loss of forty cows. A big rancher could take such a loss, but this was Sundance's only herd and he had suffered much hardship and danger to make the money to pay for it. No sign of Macdonald anywhere. Sundance talked to Francisco and one of the others about Macdonald. Both men knew why he had held back during the thirsty days; why risk getting killed when the herd looked like it was dying? Now it was different: a fine fat herd was on its way again.

Across the Concho they were stopped by a patrol of ten Texas Rangers commanded by a tough-looking honcho named Garrity. Sundance knew him by reputation only, and it was a hard one. But these were real men, leather brown and wind-burned, ready for anything that came along. Rangers could wear what they liked, but there wasn't a fancy gun rig in the log. Garrity, a sawed-off man of about forty, looked like a small rancher or a hard working foreman. All hard men, they didn't have to act tough. Garrity, an old Comanche fighter and bandit killer, was soft spoken and easy mannered. He had blue eyes and an inch of graying beard and the lobe of his right ear had been shot away sometime in the past. Still, they rode in like they meant business.

They knew where the herd was likely to cross and

they were waiting. Sundance told the old man to hold the herd against a steep bluff on the other side of the river while he heard what they wanted. He thought he knew.

No one did any talking but Garrity and he started off with an affable, "Good day to you."

Sundance nodded. "And to you. What can we do for you?"

Garrity said easily, "Mind if we take a look at your herd?"

"Help yourself," Sundance said. "You think we picked some range cows along the way?"

Garrity grinned. "Well, you know how cows get mixed in sometimes. Look, I'll be straight with you, knowing who you are. I don't think any such thing. But I got orders to check and see. No hard feelings, all right?"

"Sure," Sundance said. "Not a one."

Garrity stayed with Sundance while the Rangers nosed their horses through the herd. They were thorough but quick. One of the Rangers rode back to Garrity. "All carry the same Mexican brand, a circle with a slash from right to left. Somebody sent us on a goose hunt, Captain."

"Then we'll be on our way," Garrity said, grinning at Sundance. "You got a nice herd there. Hope you make to the north. I guess you know some people are out to stop you. Politics, they tell me. Now me, I been fighting Comanches half my life. Probably could've gone without it if the Indians had been well fed. Watch yourself, Sundance—you don't have too many friends."

Sundance grinned back at the trail-hardened Ranger. "Thanks for the kind words, Captain." He didn't say anything about Macdonald because they'd be out of Texas before long. Garrity wouldn't be able to help them then. Nobody would. They'd have to do it by their lonesome.

They crossed the Colorado and were soon in Kansas. The weather so far had been pretty good, and once they were clear of west Texas it wasn't so hot. Only a few showers had fallen, mostly in the daytime. But they were coming into a part of the country where it rained often and hard. Flooded rivers were the danger now. They crossed the Clear Fork of the Brazos and pushed on to the big river itself. Working long hours and sleeping in wet clothes, Charlie Starbright came down with a fever and chills and had to ride in the supply wagon covered by blankets. Francisco doctored him with tequila and some kind of powdered root with a terrible taste. Charlie liked the tequila and hated the medicine.

Before they reached the main Brazos, Sundance left the herd and rode on ahead. When he got to the big river the foreman of a small local herd told him they hadn't been able to ford it for ten days.

Sundance rode back to the herd, then twenty miles south of the river, and the next morning they turned the herd to the northeast, hoping to strike the Brazos a few miles above Hindman's Ferry. This was the only ferry in many days' travel, and it was the only way to get the wagons across. Sundance had to decide to wait for the river to go down or move the herd toward the ferry. It hardly mattered—time would be lost however they did it.

Sundance left the herd once it was moving in the rain and rode along the south bank of the Brazos. It rained hard and it was cold. Too much damp was as bad as too much heat, because when cows got sick on the trail they had to be left to die. Five hours later he saw the ferry through the driving rain; it was just coming back from the other shore.

The wagons got across with the help of the Swede and Con Pendleton, who then came back to help ford the herd. The current was fairly strong but the river wasn't too deep. This was their first tough crossing and every man was under strict orders to maintain his position. The approach to the crossing was gradual, but the opposite bank was steep, slick with rain and mud, with only a narrow passage to get through the flat country. Sundance took up position as point man on the right or downriver side; then with their saddle horses in the lead, they breasted the angry Brazos.

The water was shallow as they entered, but the horses were in swimming water before they got to the middle of the river. Pushed forward from the rear, the cows bawled furiously when forced to swim. Some of the lead cows began to drift and had to be headed off and set back on their course. It took half an hour to move the cattle into the water; riders already on the other side had to keep the narrow passage clear or the cows would start to pile up, fall back into the river and be swept away. The riders not clearing the passage that ran through the steep bank had to cross and re-cross the river fifteen times before the herd reached safety. By the time it did, everybody was exhausted.

But they didn't get any rest because Bowdry reported that some of the cows had found their way down into a dry arroyo. The steers had found a soft place in the bank and were disinclined to be moved out of it.

"Go easy, they're in a fighting mood," Sundance warned, as they closed in cautiously. The kneeling cattle were cutting the bank viciously with their horns and matting their heads with the red mud, with their tails curled up to show their anger. It took all the skill the men had to drive them out of there.

After leaving the river the herd was scattered over several thousand acres, grazing freely, their bellies full of water. It was best to get them settled down, so Sundance said they would let them rest all afternoon. After a while he heard the clatter of the chuckwagon as it came downriver from the ferry, Molly handling the reins like an old campaigner.

After the cattle started behaving again they got the herd into some kind of shape. The bed-ground was about a mile from the river; there were trees and plenty of deadwood for the fires. Darkness settled over the camp. It was good to have the cattle safe and a chance to dry out at the blazing fires.

The men not on guard steamed in front of the fire, glad to be on the good side of the Brazos but thinking of the food they didn't have. Sundance turned to the old man and told him to slaughter a beeve. The old man's face showed something close to shock. In cow country, odd though it was, nobody ever slaughtered a cow for food. Men on the trail herds ate just about everything but fresh meat. Day after day it was pork and beans, or thick slab bacon, or flapjacks, or son-of-a-bitch stew. Nobody ever complained about it because you didn't kill the merchandise you were driving to market.

"Just do it," Sundance ordered the old man.

"Meat that fresh is going to be a little tough. Molly probably knows how to soften it up. Go on now, Don Francisco—we're going to have a feast tonight!"

The old man had a sardonic sense of humor. Like Sundance he had a feeling that real danger wasn't far ahead. Macdonald had tried to destroy them with a poison-stampede. The drought hadn't stopped them and neither had the Brazos. There was no doubt that the Indian-hating madman would strike soon.

"All right, we'll have a meat feast," the old man said. "Or is it the Last Supper!"

Chapter Nine

The second day out from the Brazos it rained heavily during the day and drizzled during the night. Not a hoof would bed down, so the guards had to be doubled in watches for the night. Their bellies were filled, still, they were wet and miserable. Everytime Sundance turned he found Frank Pendleton staring at him. Bennington had stopped joking with the girl, which was a relief to Molly, but the Irishman was having private thoughts about her. There would be trouble there, Sundance knew, because Frank Pendleton was one of those men who could never let well enough alone. Sundance had known a lot of men like Frank; a few were still alive. Every outfit had one, sometimes even two, but the handsome Irishman was going to be worse than most. He was no kind of gunman but he was dangerous. A vain man, he wanted to be more than he was, though what he wanted to be was far from clear. Maybe the old man was right—he should have killed him!

The wet weather began to slack off but everyone was thinking about the next river they had to cross. The Wichita was hard to figure, like a flighty woman, and over the years it had been the ruination of many a good herd. If it rained again and kept at it they were in for one hell of a time.

But the weather continued dry for the next three

days, enough time for the river to fall low enough to get across. They went over late in the afternoon of the third day, and there was no more than fifty feet of swimming water. The chuckwagon gave the only trouble because there was no easy way to lighten the load. The water barrels, the empty dough barrel and a side of beef weighed it down to the water line. All mules, dependable in so many other ways, are unreliable in water; they would have to swim them across on their own or they might tumble the wagon into the river. They got the mules across first, right after the herd, and beat them into stubborn submission when they got there. Next and last came the wagon. Sundance ordered Francisco to lash the wagon box securely to the gearing with ropes. The bedding was rolled and roped to the top of the wagon where the water wouldn't get at it. Then they ran the wagon into the water by hand, and two men with guy ropes fore and aft held it steady, preventing it from toppling over. The rest of the men fastened their lariats to the end of the wagon tongue and took a wrap on their pommels with the loose end. Sundance gave the word and seven horses and men got the wagon across.

Good open country lay between the Wichita and Pease Rivers, and when they got to the Pease they found it so low they just walked the herd across. If they had reached it a week earlier they would have found it in full flood. The high-water mark could be seen on the trees along the bank. It was still May but summer freshets had to be expected. Molly, more than once, asked Sundance why she couldn't take the small supply wagon, light and fast, and head for one of the nearest towns. Some meat was left; there was no coffee. Sundance said no, though he missed strong black coffee as much as the men.

"Then where do we get fresh supplies?" Molly said angrily. "I can't cook if there's nothing to cook."

"Try fixing the meat some other way," Sundance said. "We'll get all the supplies we need at Doan's Crossing. Doan has a big trading post on the far side of the Red River."

The Red River lay dead ahead and the men were impatient to ford the herd. On the far shore, Doan ran one of the biggest stores in the West and sold whiskey on the side. Sundance decided to bed the herd when they got across and let those who wanted to get drunk. He knew the Irishmen would be the first to pull a cork. No doubt Charlie Starbright would get drunk, but it was the Pendleton brothers Sundance was thinking about; yet he knew he had to give the men a break after nearly two back-breaking months on the trail. If the Irishmen made trouble, then he would have to deal with it when it came. But they all needed a break from the monotony, a respite from sore muscles and half-numbed brains. He could move the herd on while Molly and Charlie stayed to load up on supplies. That sure as hell would make for bad feelings for the rest of the drive.

"Red River in sight!" the point man called out.

Even from a distance the Red had a big look about it. It got its name from the red bluff banks and the red mud in the water. Timber grew plentifully along its banks and the passage of a recent flood was marked by driftwood. Now it had shallowed down into several small channels that could be crossed easily.

They took the herd across, about a mile below the trading post and general store run by Patrick Henry Doan, a deceptively mild man with a great fondness for money and the sure knowledge of how to get it in the fastest possible way: keep the drovers around until their money was gone. East of the post, Doan had built a whole string of wire corrals with enough space to pen ten thousand cattle. A herd of nearly four thousand cows had moved out a few hours before Sundance got there.

Doan always came out to greet the big herds, and he came out now, affable but ever wary in a dusty black suit, a white collarless shirt, and dirt-stained Jefferson shoes. He shaved about four times a month, meaning that he had a thick stubble of beard most of the time. Sundance knew the name and the reputation, if not the man himself. Doan had a big head for such a small body and he owned three or four suits all the same cut and color, making no allowance for the heat of summer, or the cold of winter. Sundance knew he carried two .38 double-action, short-barreled Colts in the leather-lined side pockets of this coat. All his coats had leather pockets, and not only were they leather but the leather had been rubbed smooth with oil from sheeps' wool. His habit of sticking his hands in his gun pockets had given his hands a soft look. The hands of sheepherders got the same look from manhandling the woolies. But Sundance knew that Patrick Henry Doan was no shepherd. If he drove anything anywhere, it was money to the bank.

Marking Sundance for the boss of the outfit, Doan told him to make himself at home. The trader's foxy eyes took in Sundance's hardly usual appearance without a flicker of curiosity. No questions were ever asked at Doan's Crossing, and no one ever bothered Doan himself, not even the hostiles. Outlaws let him alone because he was a valuable source of supplies and information. His was the only establishment of its kind for many days' ride, and if you couldn't find it at Doan's Crossing it wasn't worth asking for. Doan asked no questions and answered none except the usual give and take about the weather, flood conditions, tick fever and the price of beef. Anything else was shrugged away as none of his business. It was rumored that he sold rifles to the Indians, but they said that about most traders.

Sundance reached down and shook hands with Doan. Francisco Aldama did the same, though he would not have done it in Mexico. The others in the outfit got quick, pleasant nods from Doan, who thought it was safe enough to crack a mild joke about Molly.

"You got yourself some cook there," Doan said. "Every outfit ought to have a cook like that."

"You can't have her," Sundance said, knowing the old man meant no harm.

Doan gave out with his old man's laugh. "Wouldn't know what to do with her if I got her. Light down, gents! First drink always on the house." Nothing was said about how long they might stay.

The trading post wasn't a single building but a lot of buildings joined together with passageways and doors. Doan added space to meet the demands of business, and every year the sprawl of buildings grew larger and uglier, until now it had reached the size of a small village. Doan, or somebody, had a sense of humor, because signs were nailed up all over the place, identifying Delmonico's Hotel, New York City, Buckingham Palace, The Very Grand Canyon, and Special Baths for Ladies. On most days it bustled with business; today, it drowsed in the hot sun on the edge of the prairie. It smelled of coffee sacks, salt pork, leather goods, gun oil, saddle soap, sweat, beer and cow shit.

Inside the low-roofed main building it was hard to see after the glare of the sun. Molly, holding a list of supplies, came in after Sundance and Francisco. The other men still were putting the herd in the corrals. Knowing Doan's reputation, Sundance had warned Molly to be sure everything she bought was put in the supply wagon. At Doan's it was not unknown for part of the supplies to be unloaded after the driver got drunk.

Doan took the sheet of paper from Molly and complimented her on her handwriting. Molly ignored the old man's flattery. "I'll check everything off as it goes into the wagon," she said.

Doan was a glib old bastard. "To be sure," he said. "At P.H. Doan's, the customer is always right." He whistled and a fat white woman with some Indian in her came out from behind a stack of rifle crates. Doan told her to get started on the list of supplies. Then he turned to Sundance. "Now sir, about the drink you been waiting for. Barroom is right this way."

Francisco smiled at Sundance and said "zorro" to Doan's back. Doan turned with a pleased grin. "I heard that, senor. Sure I'm a fox, but now I got my own chicken coop." Doan looked distressed that Molly wasn't joining them in the bar. "Ain't the cookie coming?" he asked.

Molly snapped back at him, not a bit taken in by

his wily ways. "Don't you call me 'cookie,' Granddad. Somebody forgot to invite me."

"You're invited," Sundance said.

The bar was in a building by itself, a low-roofed, plank-walled room with the skulls of longhorns and other critters nailed up behind the wood. The head of a bighorn sheep stood out from all the rest, and Sundance knew that Doan must have taken it in trade for something. Old Glory and the thistle flag of Scotland were crossed and dusty above the bar. The bar itself was rough and planked like the walls, but the top had been worn smooth by bottles and glasses and rough hands. A flaking mirror advertising Old Crow whiskey reflected light from the hanging lanterns. There were windows but they were small and narrow, and could be shuttered quickly for an Indian attack. The bar was well stocked for such a remote place, but since there were no pumps or ice, the beer was in bottles and it was warm. Missing from the whole collection was a framed first-dollar-I-ever-made; ten to one, it was in the bank with all Doan's other dollars.

"I sure as hell do," Doan said cheerfully when Francisco asked if he had tequila. "And none of your poison neither. Even got some Mexican rum could be taken for a fair brandy."

Molly had ordered a bottle of Pearl Beer and was drinking it. It frothed high in the glass mug and she blew off the head. Doan was pleased when she ordered another bottle right on top of the first. He was disappointed when Sundance didn't ask for anything but a bottle of the same beer. Francisco got salt and lemon and knocked his tequila back with a sign of satisfaction. Doan, smiling happily as coins clinked on the bar, set him up again.

"Sure is a nice day," Doan said, removing the empty beer bottles.

Francisco nodded agreement, with the second glass to his lips. Sundance said it was a fine day. Molly, not in such good humor, asked what was no nice about it. Without waiting for an answer, she ordered another bottle of Pearl. The men began to come in, all but the Swede and Charlie Starbright, who were going to keep the first watch on the corraled cattle. Sundance knew Doan was too smart to rustle any cattle from his own corrals. Even so, he was going to post two men at all times, as a reminder.

The three *vaqueros* got a bottle of tequila and sat apart at a table pushed against the wall. Except for the old man, they seldom spoke to anyone. They spoke English when they had to; they didn't advertise it. Bennington, wanting to prove that he was no dude, asked for the worst rotgut he could think of. Doan had it. No Irish whiskey was available for the Pendleton brothers, and they had to make do with a dusty bottle of Scotch.

Bennington had been to Scotland and wanted to talk to Doan about it. "What part do you hail from?" he wanted to know.

"All over and not lately," Doan answered. "You're right though. Scotland is a fine country, or so they tell me."

In five minutes the Pendleton brothers had put away three big drinks of whiskey and were working on the fourth. Con Pendleton looked over at Doan, standing with both hands flat on the bar. "I think Scotland is a stinking country," he said. "It's lousy and it stinks."

Doan turned his old man's eyes toward the Irishman. "Sure," he said. "Why not!"

Nursing their tequila, the *vaqueros* looked to Francisco Aldama for guidance, but got no response. Sundance drank some more of the warm beer. Iced or warm, Pearl was the tastiest beer in the Southwest.

Con Pendleton knocked back his whiskey, wiped his mouth and made a smear on his dusty face. "The hell with Scotland," he said. "Ireland is the only real country."

"You betcha," Doan said, whose only nation was the bank; his flag the dollar sign.

Taking no heed of his brother's patriotic outburst, Frank Pendleton was staring at Molly standing between the old man and Sundance. Molly had washed her face and brushed her hair before coming in from the corrals.

"Hey Doan," Frank started. "You got any music around this place? I feel like dancing."

Reaching down, the Scotsman dragged an unfastened concertina up from behind the bar. It made a long wheezing note as it came up and was set on the bar. "All I got," Doan said. "What would you like, boy? A jig or a reel?"

"Jigs and reels my ass!" Frank said, as if he had been called an Irish clodhopper mick. "Play us a nice waltz if you know how to play a nice waltz. Not too fast and not too slow, you understand. I don't like them when they're too fast or too slow."

Doan nodded. "My own sentiments entirely," he said. "How does this sound to you?"

Frank Pendleton listened solemnly while the trader squeezed out a few bars of some old tune. "A little faster, Doan," the Irishman said. "That's more like it."

Con Pendleton, still preoccupied with thoughts of the Old Sod, raised his glass. "Here's to the Emerald Isle," he declared. He didn't seem to mind that nobody joined in the toast.

Here it comes, Sundance decided, as Frank Pendleton belted back his sixth drink and stood up whacking the dust from his clothes with his hat. The handsome clodhopper threw his hat on the table and ran his fingers through his coal black hair; oily black after many weeks without a wash. Molly knew he was coming up behind her, but she kept her back turned.

"Would you care to dance, Molly me love?" Frank Pendleton asked.

Still not turning, Molly told him to go jump himself. Bennington smiled but no one else did. The *vaqueros* sat silent. The Irishman's red face flamed redder and he raised his voice. "Well, if I did that, Molly me love, then I'd have no use for you. Would I?"

Doan watched over the top of his concertina.

Molly reached for her beer the same time that Frank grabbed at her arm and some of the beer got spilled. Now when she turned she had the almost empty bottle in her hand. "I wouldn't dance with you for the Denver Mint," she said. "Grab me again and I'll split your goddamned skull. I mean it, paddy!"

Doan put down the concertina and reminded Sundance that he'd have to pay for any damage to his place. "They charge me extry for the beer bottles," he said.

Faced with Molly's wrath, the Irishman began to wheedle, for the moment trying to make his point with blarney instead of force. "Ah, where's the harm in a little dance?" he said. "It won't kill you and might do you good."

Bennington bolted a glass of rotgut and tried not to shudder as it went down to burn his belly. The artist was big enough, had been a marksman and athlete at college. He grinned at the soft-soaping Irishman. "Why don't you dance with me, Frank?"

Sundance turned at last. "Frank doesn't want to dance with you, he wants to dance with me. That's what this is all about, isn't it, Frank?"

The whiskey was working on the Irishman; this time he wasn't going to back down. "Maybe it is," he said. "I just wanted to dance with Molly and you have to butt in. What gives you the right to do that, may I ask?"

"Might makes right," Sundance said calmly. "Leave Molly alone and go drink your drink. No big deal here—Molly doesn't feel like dancing."

Molly stared at Sundance. "Nobody asked you to stick up for me."

Sundance told her to shut up.

Frank Pendleton laughed. "That's telling him, Molly me love. Come on, now, let's take a few turns of the ballroom. Get that squeeze-box working, Doan."

The trader knew the festivities had been suspended, if not entirely over. "The band went home," he said.

Smiling, Frank Pendleton held out his arms to Molly, then tried to slip them around her waist. She pushed hard and he staggered and when he regained his balance Sundance had pushed Molly to one side.

"Drop it, Frank," Sundance said. This wasn't

mutiny on the trail; no need for killing. He hoped there wasn't.

Con Pendleton got up and stood beside his brother. They both grinned at Sundance and kept their hands away from their guns. Even with all the whiskey in them, they knew they couldn't beat him to the draw. And they knew, too, that he wouldn't do any killing unless they started it.

"I think we better have it out," Frank said at last.

"Not in here," Doan said, putting one hand in his pocket.

Frank grinned again. "The only thing is, you got to take on the two of us. It's like we're twins, you understand. You're a great big fierce man with a terrible reputation for violence. You won't mind taking on two amateurs, will you now? We'll just leave our guns and knives with Mr. Doan here, and you do the same. It'll be a fair fight, fair enough anyhow. Why is it suddenly you got nothing to say? A big fierce terrible fella such as you are."

Sundance knew he could kill the two Pendletons with two shots, heart or head. That would be as simple as finishing his beer. Going against them with his fists would't be simple at all. Both Pendletons were young, work-hardened and tough, the product of railroad gangs and no end of saloon brawls. They were Irishman, not as wild as some but wilder than others, and like most Irishmen they liked fighting for its own sake. He knew they were sure they could beat him, and maybe they were right. But if he didn't end the trouble here and now it would fester like an unhealed wound.

"Let's go outside," he said.

Chapter Ten

Doan said the best place for the fight would be the empty horse corral. On the way there he made a stab at restoring peace, then gave up when he saw that an end to the trouble might be better for business.

"Later I hope you fellas will shake and make up," Doan said hopefully. "Then you can get down to real drinking. The men watching the herd ain't even wet their whistles yet."

Their weapons had been left behind on the bar and before they went out to fight, Doan explained that one of the main rules of the house called for the immediate killing of any man who held out on a hidden gun or knife.

Francisco Aldama didn't approve of any of it, but he went too, with the three *vaqueros* trailing behind. Mexicans of any kind didn't like fighting with their fists; such combat was womanish and without honor. The old man spoke quietly to Sundance. "If it goes against you, what do you want me to do?"

"Nothing," Sundance said. "If they beat me I'll just have to take it. No killing, old friend. You want me to make that an order?"

The old man nodded. "I will obey you if you make it an order."

Sundance said, "Then that's what it is. This is Doan's place, let him handle it."

They faced off in the center of the big corral armed with nothing but their fists and feet. And their teeth? Sundance knew the Pendletons might be "rippers," as they were called in the wild Irish railroad gangs. A lot of noses and ears had been lost in fights with rippers. He had no doubt that they would try to gouge his eyes out.

"No weapons, no rules," Doan said before he backed off.

Except for the lazy bawling of the herd, it was hot and quiet in the empty corral. The *vaqueros* drifted in to stand behind the old man; Molly and Bennington stood alone, the artist with his sketch pad, the girl with a bottle of beer.

The Pendletons had stripped down to pants and boots; Sundance took off his hat and shirt. The Irishman stared at the old scars criss-crossing Sundance's belly and chest. Some had been made by bullets and knives; most were the result of his boyhood initiation into Cheyenne warriorship.

Sundance knew he had to keep them in front of him, if he could. But he knew that wouldn't be possible all the time. Con was bigger and stronger than Frank, but Frank was faster on his feet, and maybe more vicious. To Con, it was just another brawl; Frank, for his part, would fight like a wildcat because Molly was there.

"Come and get it, boss," Frank said, beckoning to Sundance.

Sundance stayed where he was and the instant they began to move he saw they fought as a team. Frank on the right, his brother on the left. Waiting for them to close in, Sundance tensed and then relaxed. To win, you had to believe in your brain and gut that you could do it. No, it was more than that: you had to will yourself to win, you had to push aside all doubt. There was no conceit in this, simply iron-willed determination. In the great fighting days of the Cheyenne he had been taught this by the fiercest fighter of all, Spotted Pony, who had taught him to show no fear—and no mercy.

Frank Pendleton threw a casual righthand punch at Sundance to get the feel of the man he was fighting. Sundance dodged it as easily as it was thrown. Con edged in to take his own measure. Then, as if by a signal, they came at him together in a whirlwind of blows intended to drop him in the first minute of the fight. Sundance jumped to one side and kicked Con in the kneecap. Bunched together, his toes struck home with the force of a club. Con yelled with pain and he staggered but didn't go down. Frank, red-faced with anger, landed a punch to Sundance's jaw, then danced away as Sundance lashed out at him with the other foot.

Con was moving back in but not with the same confidence. He stomped his heavy boots to get the feeling back in his leg. "Oh, it's going to be like that, is it? We got ourself a kicker, Frankie!"

They rushed in again trying to overpower him with their ferocity and brute strength. Con came in head-on while Frank tried to move to the side. Frank yelled but Sundance didn't turn as Con rushed in with his head down, trying for a butt in the belly. Con had his head down and his fists balled like buffers on a train. Sundance let him come all the way before he grabbed Con's fists and pulled him forward, dropping on his back at the same time. Gripping Con's fists securely, flat on his back, Sundance brought up his feet and threw Con fifteen feet into the air. Con yelled as he went up and came down with a crash. Before Sundance could roll out of the way, Frank came in kicking and landed two kicks in the ribs. If Sundance hadn't been moving when the kicks landed, his ribcage would have been crushed. Con was back on his feet but limping badly, his fists bunched like oak knots, his face dark with dirt and anger. Sundance went after Frank to draw Con in on him. Sundance made a great show of wanting to get at Frank, but he was waiting for Con. Con was a lot more careless than Frank, because he didn't care what happened to his face. The vain one, Frank wanted to keep his face pretty for the girls, and that was going to get him into trouble. Going hard for the face, Sundance drove Frank back with his fists. Con was faster than he'd figured because out of nowhere he got a punch to the back of the neck that might have ended the fight if he had been a weaker man. As it was, he had to fight defensively for a minute or so until his head cleared up. Heartened by Con's mankilling punch, Frank attacked from the other side, and by sheer energy they forced him back. He backed off fast until he had enough space to make a run at Con, then he sprang into the air and kicked Con in the chest with both feet. Con went down again and while he was struggling to get up Sundance kicked him in the face. That didn't stop him but it slowed him. Frank landed a punch to Sundance's belly that drove the wind out of him. Con bowled Sundance over with a rush and tried to drop his weight on top of him. If one could pin him down, the other could cripple him with kicks. Con sprang at Sundance but landed on nothing but dirt. Then before Con could move or Frank could cover for his brother, Sundance jumped and came down with his heels digging into Con's kidneys. The Irishman screamed as Sundance's heels, tough as whang leather, struck the small of his back at the same time. Con lay writhing in agony, clawing at the dirt, while Sundance turned to concentrate his attack on Frank. Con was out of it for a while, and now it was Frank's turn.

Faced with Sundance, Frank showed fear for the first time. But he was no coward, Sundance knew. Against anyone else he would have been a formidable opponent, but he had no way of knowing the man he was fighting. If he had, he might have walked the other way. Any sensible man would have, because here was a man who knew the meaning of mercy but ignored it when he had to.

For a while they were fairly well matched; many weeks on the trail had hammered the Irishman into top fighting condition. Sundance looked for chances to use his feet, but didn't find any. Some of his surprises had been used up, but there were others. Frank guessed there were and kept trying to anticipate where the next one would come from.

Frank launched an attack that drove Sundance back toward Con, still moaning in the dirt. Suddenly he felt Con's hand grip his right heel and hang on hard. Now was Frank's turn to make a killing assault. Sundance raised his left foot and kicked back at Con's face and heard his nose snap. Frank hit him a solid blow in the face at the same time. Sundance fell but as he did Con's hold was broken and he rolled free before Frank could get him with his boots.

Up again with a trickle of blood at the corner of his mouth, Sundance knew that Con was no longer a threat. Con lay with his hands pressed over his streaming nose, cursing like a madman, but completely out of action. Frank began to circle Sundance, at the same time trying to keep away from him. Sundance turned as Frank turned, and then when Frank had maneuvered himself into facing the sun, Sundance attacked with blows to the head and belly that bewildered the other man. Long ago he had mastered the art of fighting with both hands delivering almost equal punishment, and this was something new to the Irishman, who like most men favored one hand over the other. Frank's right was powerful but he didn't know how to use his left. Sundance switched back and forth from right to left hand until the Irishman was reeling under the impact of his blows. It would be no disgrace for Frank to cash in his chips, to fall down under the force of the onslaught, yet he kept fighting to the end.

It came quickly; even quicker than Sundance expected. He was tired himself but knew he could kept on going if he had to. Frank had guts but lacked the dogged will to win. Sundance hit him again and kept on hitting and now the best Frank could do was try to cover his face. Every time he raised his fists in front of his face, Sundance pounded him in the belly. He could have kicked his feet from under him; there was no longer any need. There would be a better finish to the fight if he didn't use his feet. Sundance drew Frank's fists away from his face and then standing flat footed he delivered a right hand punch to the jaw that snapped the Irishman's head back. Still he lurched forward again and Sundance had to hit him again, putting all his strength behind the blow, sick of it now, wanting to get it over with. Frank Pendleton fell down and didn't move.

Doan came hurrying from the gate of the corral with the part-Indian fat woman waddling behind him with a bottle of whiskey in one hand, a bucket of water in the other. Francisco Aldama and his *vaqueros* drifted over as if nothing much had happened. Molly carried another bucket and a handful of torn sheet.

Doan rubbed his soft hands together without making a sound. "Well now sir, that was one tidy little ruckus, weren't it. Many's a one I seen in this old corral but never any jumping like you did."

Only Bennington was excited, and more by his artwork than by the fight. He had done a whole series of quick sketches while the fight was in progress. The woman offered Sundance the bottle and he rinsed out his bleeding mouth with a slug of whiskey. The woman and Molly began to work on the groaning Irishmen. Francisco Aldama was reluctant to take any active part in these dishonorable proceedings.

Bennington shoved the sketch pad at Sundance. "That's you jumping in mid-air. I think I caught it right but I'm not sure. I don't mean now but some time when you have time, would you mind jumping like that again?"

Sundance told him to go to hell and went over to look at the men he had downed. Con Pendleton was tough and strong and he guessed a good kick in the kidneys wouldn't kill him, even if he pissed red for a week. Doan yelled at two of his hired men to bring an old door so they could carry Con back into the bar. Frank, not beaten half so badly, was still out cold. Frown-faced, Molly stood over him and poured the bucket of water over his face until he started to gag and splutter.

Frank opened his eyes and looked up at Sundance. "Christ Almighty! What was that last thing you hit me with?"

"How are you feeling, Frank?" Sundance asked. "You wouldn't fall down, so I had to hit you with everything I had. You're an Irishman, you ought to understand that."

Frank felt his jaw and his nose before he answered. "Nothing banged up too bad. What did you say? You hear me complaining, did you?"

"Not so far."

"And you won't. Gimme a hand up, will you boss?"

Sundance reached out his left hand to help the conceited Irishman to his feet. If he tried anything he would put him back to sleep with the other hand. But if any hate remained it didn't show in the Irishman's battered face. He stuck out his hand and Sundance shook it, thinking how crazy men were.

"There's always a better man," Frank said. "When you go around asking for something you usually get it. Will you look at old Con there with the women fussing over him! Don't worry about him. Nothing will kill that man but the strong drink. Speaking of which. . ."

The fat woman gave Frank the bottle and he drank like the thirsty man he was. Just then Sundance saw Doan shading his eyes with his hand, as a stringbean rider on a black horse came from the direction of the Red River. Doan darted a quick look at Sundance before he allowed that he'd better get back to the store. Sundance watched while the old Scotsman went into the store followed by the rider, who just threw his reins over the rail in a careless hitch.

They got Con on the door and carried him back into the barroom, where the fat woman now tended bar instead of Doan. Doan and the rider had gone into some other part of the sprawl of buildings. Prodded by his brother, Con agreed to shake hands with Sundance before he groaned his way off the door and sat heavily in a chair. Sundance thought the handshake was real enough, but Frank thought it was lacking in spirit.

Carrying a bottle to the table, he said angrily, "I won't drink with you till you congratulate the man. Go on now, do it, you Irish son of a bitch!"

Con sucked at the first drink through bloody lips. "You beat us good. I'd as soon go up against John L. himself than square off with you again."

"A truer word was never spoken," his brother agreed, including everybody in his beaming smile. "Fighting is like drinking in a way." He groaned, still smiling. "Great fun while you're at it, but you have to pay the price. But the fighting man goes on fighting as the drinking man goes on drinking."

Sundance had had his drink, so he pushed the bottle across the table to Frank. "Don't go on fighting with me, Frank."

"Hell no! I didn't mean that. Only a cur keeps on trying to get the advantage of the man has bested him in a fair fight. I'm talking about fights in the future."

Francisco Aldama muttered, "Such crazy men! And you, senor the boss, are no less crazy."

Sundance smiled. "You wouldn't understand, you're not Irish."

"For which I thank the Creator," the old man said, but he smiled, too.

Sundance looked up and saw Doan beckoning him from the doorway of one of the storerooms. Francisco saw that he was included in the beckon and followed Sundance. As they left, Frank Pendleton was trying to interest Bennington in a sketch of what the Irishman described as "the noble but defeated gladiator."

Doan led the way into the darkened storeroom where the stringbean rider sat on a nail keg with a bottle of beer in his hand. It didn't take more than one look for Sundance to peg him for what he was, an outlaw, a longrider. He was taller than Sundance but without the copper-skinned halfbreed's lithe grace. He wore a long-barreled Army Colt .45 in a greased, open-ended holster on a plain black belt. He let the old man do the talking.

Doan turned. "First off, you got to give me your word you never seen this fella."

Sundance spoke for both of them. "You got it."

"Then say hello to Stretch Glazer," the old man said.

"Gents!" the lanky outlaw said with a brief nod.

Sundance had seen wanted posters on the outlaw in a few places. Murder, cattle stealing, stage robbery, passing counterfeit money for some city gang back East. He guessed Glazer was pretty bad news; mostly it showed in his pale, cold, almost-yellow eyes.

Doan was too worried to sit down, and that wasn't like him. Come hell or high water, drought or floods, the old man turned a beady-eyed foxily smiling face to the world. Now he dropped the crusty old codger pose and talked straight for a change, no longer stumbling over his words with the care he usually took.

"Stretch here says Larch Macdonald is going to hit your herd. Hit it tonight if you stay over. Hit it late today if you decide to move on. That's the straight of it, Sundance. Me and Stretch are old friends from way back and he wouldn't lie to me. One hand washes the other. I scratch Stretch's back and he does mine. You believe me or not?"

"You're telling it, Doan."

"Damn right I am. Now you're wondering why should Stretch Glazer go out of his way to give me this information. Simple! Stretch doesn't want me to think he has any part of it. Him or his boys. Up here the law isn't looking too hard for Stretch and everybody gets along fine. Stretch and me have certain profitable business deals worked out. Forget about that and let him tell his story."

"Sure," Sundance said.

The outlaw had a high voice to go with his six feet, four inches, but there was nothing funny about it. "You know Macdonald is out to stop you. Ought to. Everybody else does. Macdonald wasn't back in the country a month before everybody knew it. I heard he was heading up this way but didn't figure he'd try to hit you at Pat's Crossing. So I figured what he did to you was none of my business."

The old man cut in. "Stretch changed his mind. Simple! Macdonald got word to Stretch that he'd cut him in for the whole herd if he brought his boys along on the raid. Don't tell me you wasn't tempted, Stretch, old fella!"

"Not that much," Glazer said. "Cow stealing is cumbersome work for a wanted man. Besides, I wouldn't want to get you mad at me."

"Damn right!" the old man said. "And not just me. Word got out you did me dirt you'd have every outlaw in the Southwest gunning for you. You got the good sense not to shit where you eat. Macdonald don't give a good goddamn 'cause he's no kind of regular outlaw. Why in hell couldn't he stay down in Old Mexico instead of coming up here bothering hard-working businessmen."

The old man had talked himself into a temper. "I been squatting in this place twenty-three years now and nothing like this ever happened before. Live and let live, is what I say. Do your robbing and murdering some other place away from here. That's the rule. That *was* the rule till Macdonald came along."

Sundance held up his hand. "You talk too much, Doan. Tell us now, what's it going to be? Are you warning us or offering help or what?" Though Stretch Glazer's story had the ring of truth, he wasn't sure that the whole thing might not be intended to catch him off guard. An old man who ran with killers and outlaws was capable of most anything. Maybe not. A man like Doan wasn't likely to bend the law too hard because there was more money in not bending it.

Doan looked surprised. "What do you think it's going to be? We'll fight the son of a bitch, catch him by surprise when he comes. Just don't count on any help from anybody but me, Patrick Henry Doan."

Sundance looked at Glazer for confirmation of

this. He got it. "Can't help you," Glazer said. "Even the boys don't know I'm up here today. Had to ride like a bastard to get here. But that's as far as it goes. Macdonald may be crazy but he's an outlaw just like me. Like the boys. Sorry Sundance, you'll have to handle him yourself."

Doan slapped the outlaw on his narrow, bony shoulder. "You don't have to be sorry, Stretch. You done me a nice favor coming here and I won't forget you for it. Better get back now before some of your boys catch on."

A few minutes later Sundance said, "Funny thing you don't tell us to move the herd, Doan." Francisco nodded in silent agreement, one old man with no trust in the other.

Doan took one of the Colt .38's from his pocket and spun the cylinder. "Would you go if I did? Didn't think you would. You have a better chance here than out on the open prairie. You have a better chance now that you know about it. You want the hard truth, Sundance? Which is, I don't give a shit about this trouble between you and Macdonald. It's me I'm thinking about. Me and my fat woman out there—but mostly me."

"Your reputation would be tarnished, is that it?"

"Such as it is, it would. Blame Patrick Henry Doan for everything is how it goes in this part of the country. You lose your herd in this vicinity and they'll whisper I was in on it. Then word gets out and pretty soon the drovers will stop coming."

Sundance said, "Three thousand head might be worth a little mud-slinging."

The foxy Scotsman laughed while he checked the loads in the other stubby revolver. "Bless you sonny, I got enough money to buy twenty or thrity herds bigger'n yours. No sir, you stay right here and I'm going to help you whip that Canuck son of a bitch's bastard!'' Doan squinted at the narrow window. "Got ourself a few hours left by the way the sun lays right now. Larch Macdonald is going to be sorry he ever tangled with Patrick Henry Doan. Too bad you beat up so hard on those Irishmen. That one you jumped on don't look too good from where I stand."

"They'll fight all right when the time comes."

Patrick Henry Doan, money-grubber and associate of outlaws, laughed hard enough to bust a gut, and not for a moment did he show the slightest sign of fear. He stopped laughing and grinned at Sundance. "They'd better fight," he said. "It's either that or get buried. You, me—everybody!"

Chapter Eleven

"We have to make it look like the party's going to go on all night," Sundance said. "That's the one chance we have—surprise."

Bennington nodded his agreement but he frowned too. "How are we going to do that and guard the herd at the same time?"

"The best way we can," Sundance said. "Doan, can your lady play the concertina?"

"Near as good as I can," the Scotsman answered. "She can shoot a rifle just as good."

Sundance said the main thing was to keep the herd intact. By itself, beating off a raid wouldn't be that hard now that they were warned. But if Macdonald managed to run off the herd during the fight, then he would have accomplished a big part of what he was trying to do. After thinking about it, he guessed that Macdonald would try to scatter the herd into the wild Indian Lands that lay ahead. For many miles to the north lay rough, broken country slashed by gullies and ravines. Out there it would take weeks to round up what was left of the herd and that would mean breaking up the outfit into small parties; easy prey for Macdonald's gunmen. Even if they did manage to work under sniper fire, they couldn't expect to gather up more than half the herd. They would lose the rest to marauding Indians and rustlers, to drought and fire and ranchers with a long rope. Some of the cattle would run themselves to death, or they would lie broken-backed at the bottom of deep ravines.

"We can't do much while it's still light," Sundance said. "No way to tell if they're watching us from way off. My guess is they are. That's what I'd do if I went after a big herd. Get the windows open, Doan. You or somebody. I want to be sure the sound of the music travels."

Doan called his hired men, two oldtimers, and told them to air out the place. One had a peg-leg and the other was half blind. "Don't count on Ez and Maxwell," Doan said. "They're too old. Me, it's different. I'm just a boy."

Sundance glanced at the two old men. "They can make noise," he said. "Sing and make noise." He looked at Con Pendleton sitting with his brother at one of the tables.

"I'm all right," the Irishman said quickly. "I don't want to make noise with two old men. Right now I'm a bit slow but you just set me in a nice place and I'll be fine."

During the day, the guard on the cows had been changed three times. Short watches were the usual thing when a herd was held over near a town. That way everybody got a chance to have a few drinks and to buy supplies of their own.

"They'll come from the river, from the south," Francisco Aldama said. "I think they'll hit us from there."

"Makes sense," Sundance said. "They split their force. One party will break up the party, the other will run off the herd. Macdonald will figure that he can keep us pinned down in here. He'll be expecting only a light guard on the herd. Nobody ever stole a cow at Doan's Crossing unless Doan stole it himself."

"That ain't nice, Sundance." But Doan was pleased.

Sundance said, "That's a compliment, Doan. It's never been done and that's why Macdonald is doing it. This is a secure place so he figures we'll feel the same way. It'll be dark in an hour and I'd like to hear some music."

Doan said, "Coming up as ordered." The fat woman came when called and she picked up the concertina without a word. Sundance hadn't heard a word from her all day; he hoped she'd make a lot more noise when the time came.

"Play everything you know and keep on playing," Doan said. "Sing loud, you old tub of lard." The Scotman's tone was fond. He stabbed a finger at the two old men who stood waiting for orders. "Sing, you old bastards! Sing hard or I'll dock your wages!" To get them in the spirit of the thing, Doan sang himself:

"*And the pony-horse she do get shy,
When bitten by the Bluetail Fly!*"

The two old men began to sing, bewildered by the danger that had come to their safe corner of the world, understanding only half of it. Doan, singing hard himself, urged them on with yips and screeches. The noise was awful; just about right. The old man with the peg-leg was a better, a louder, singer than his partner. But they both did all right and they brightened up considerably when Sundance told the Scotsman to give them whiskey.

"They don't need it," Doan said. "But I'll take the money for their old age."

"Give them the whiskey," Sundance said. "Francisco and I are going out to walk around."

Outside, the noise-making sounded good. At first the herd got restless but the cows settled down after they got used to it. In the west the sky was a mass of red clouds and it was getting dark. Unless they were very close, Macdonald's watchers wouldn't be able to see them in a few minutes.

Francisco said, "We could be wrong about Macdonald coming from the south." Now that danger was near the old Mexican was a lot livelier, as if he couldn't wait for it to get even closer.

Sundance said, "We could be wrong but we have to bet on the south. Our force is too small to cover everything. We're in a big game, old friend, and we have to play it big."

"How big?"

"We leave the herd unguarded and hope the corral will hold them when the shooting starts. They can't be too gun-shy after all the shooting they heard on the way here."

"That's possible. But if they run it will be the same as if Macdonald scattered them. Macdonald can just fade away and let them run. You must decide."

"We leave the herd unguarded," Sundance said. "A few more guns could make the difference at the river. That's where we're going to do it. When they're right in the middle of the river. We'll divide our force and catch them in the middle."

"God willing," the old Mexican said as they turned to stroll back to the store, two men talking quietly in the dusk of the evening. The light was all but gone when they got there. Inside the noise was still going on. The two old men were singing as if their lives depended on it, and they did. The rest of the outfit was armed and ready.

"It's time," Sundance said. "You Charlie, go fetch the men guarding the herd."

Doan raised his bushy eyebrows but said nothing. The noise of the party followed them as Doan led the way through the sprawl of buildings and then out into near-darkness. They couldn't hear the river because of the noise. There was no moon yet but Doan said the sky looked like there would be one later. Sundance thought so too. They waited until they were joined by Francisco's *vaqueros,* the last guard on the herd.

"First they'll listen, then they'll come across." Sundance said the plan of ambush was simple. "Half go across, half stay here. Francisco will go across with his men. Lindermann and Bennington will go with them. The rest of us will stay." Sundance didn't tell Molly that she didn't have to take part in it, because every rifle and six-shooter was going to count.

"I'll stay on this side," Doan said, thinking of his store.

Darkness grew thicker as they eased their way down to the river, not going directly but spreading out across the north bank. In the channel where the ford was the water was shallow, but down from there it was deep enough. Closer to the river they could hear the rush of the water and the noise it made in the shallow places. Con Pendleton grunted with pain as he walked and Sundance told him to pick any place he liked on the north bank.

A patch of rocks and brush grew to the right of

the crossing and the Irishman eased himself down behind it. "Right in the front row," he whispered hoarsely.

Francisco and the others didn't all cross the river at the same place. Macdonald and his men might have taken up their positions on the other side. Probably not, Sundance thought. Not with horses. He guessed they would ride to the river, making as little noise as possible, then scout the trading post before they crossed. There was no need to tell Francisco to kill the wounded; in Mexico the wounded always got killed.

The banks of the river sloped down on both sides; firing from above would keep them from getting hit by their own fire. In the river the water ran fast in the darkness. Sundance looked up at the sky and the last of the red glow was gone. A wind blew along the river and it still was hot from the heat of the day. Sundance told the men on his side not to spread out too far. If they wanted to concentrate their fire, they would have to stay closer together. For a while he could see the shapes of Francisco and the others in the river. Then darkness swallowed them and there was no sound except for the rush of the water. Behind them, past the trading post, the herd moved uneasily in the corral, sensing that something was wrong. This was the first time the cows had been left untended and it made them nervous. The sound of the concertina and the singing drifted down from the store wrecking the peace of the dark night air. Doan had set out extra lamps and the barroom blazed with light. A ringtail snuffled its way along the bank of the river; only its white-banded tail showed in the darkness. Then the animal caught wind of them and ran under a narrow ledge. They had good cover where they were; under the cottonwoods that lined the river it was darker than out in the open. Branches creaked in the wind and the grass rustled along the banks of the river. The attack could come at any time, in a few minutes or just before dawn. Lying with the Winchester pushed out in front of him, Sundance looked up at the night sky and the rolling clouds. The moon came up behind the clouds and the light was better but still not good enough. The cows had settled down a little though the twang of the wire as they pushed against it could be heard faintly above the sound of the music. A few minutes later, he heard them coming.

Sundance knew that none of the others had heard it yet. When the wind faded so did the sound, and then it came back. Horses and men moving cautiously in the dark. Clouds still tumbled their way across the sky, shutting off most of the light. The sounds of the muffled hoofs grew louder, at least to Sundance, and then he heard movement under the trees as the others heard them too.

The clouds parted and the river was black and wide in the moonlight. Sundance could see them now. They had brought their horses to a walk and were edging down to the bank of the river. Something in their movements made Sundance think of blindmen. They rode in a bunch so there was no way to tell which one was Larch Macdonald. If they could kill Macdonald they would have to face other killers but their chances would be better. Other killers would do it just for the money; they would lack Macdonald's crazed determination. It was hard to count them in a bunch. Sundance guessed about twenty or twenty-five. All mean men because Macdonald didn't ride with any other kind. He hoped one of the Irishmen didn't get wild and start shooting before the time was right.

Macdonald and his men waited a few minutes before they started across. The moon was reflected in the dark water of the river, its shape bent by the fast-moving current. Moonlight glinted on the barrels of their drawn guns. Macdonald had them under good discipline and they crossed at a steady pace, with no rider trying to outdistance the others. It still wasn't possible to identify Macdonald; sighting on a big man on a big horse, Sundance hoped it might be him.

He squeezed the trigger and the rifle jetted flame. The big man pitched off his horse. Sundance swung the Winchester and blew another rider from the saddle. Then from both sides of the river they opened up. Macdonald's men were yelling as lead poured into them. A riderless horse plunged downstream into deeper water. The solid mass of raiders came apart and some rode forward, six-shooters blazing; some tried to go back.

In the first minute of shooting, about half of Macdonald's men were killed or wounded. They could have finished all of them if the clouds hadn't rolled over the moon. A hoarse voice was yelling at the raiders to get upstream. He didn't know what Macdonald sounded like but knew that had to be it. And he loosed a whole load of shells at the sound. Bullets came back at him but were fired too fast and went high. Horses splashed wildly in the shallows and Sundance jumped to his feet and ran along the bank, firing as he went. Yelling like a madman, Frank Pendleton ran behind. On the far bank Francisco's men were running too. Gunsmoke hung over the river like a fog now that the wind had died. The raiders still were in the river, but now they were getting away, no longer returning fire. Hoofs clattered over rocks in the shallows and far down Sundance heard the heave and grunt of horses being forced up the bank of the river. North or south? He didn't know and it made no difference: they had done all the killing they were going to do that night.

Sundance stopped running and ordered the men to fall back. They called out their names and no one had been killed, though Frank Pendleton had a slight bullet crease along his ribs. Francisco and the others crossed the river and they all moved back to the herd. Now that the firing had stopped, the wheeze of the concertina came from the trading post, and old Doan began to laugh.

"Dumb! Dumb! Dumb!" he said. "They played and sang all through the fight. I better go tell them to stop."

The herd was still penned in spite of broken wire and uprooted fence posts. Charlie Starbright and the *vaqueros* moved along the side of the corral talking softly to the cattle. Back down at the house the concertina gave out with one last dismal note, and then it stopped for good.

Sundance ordered the rest of the outfit to fan out from the corral, to take up their positions in case Macdonald came back for another attack. Sundance didn't think he would. They had inflicted heavy losses on the raiders, but you couldn't count on what Macdonald would do. If an attack came, all they could do was to be ready for it. The herd would have to stay where it was until morning. One way or another, it was going to be a long night.

A century seemed to pass before first light streaked the sky with gray. Gray turned to red and the sun flooded the country with light. Sundance stood up and told the others they could come out; one by one they emerged, yawning and stretching, some smiling like Frank Pendleton. Even the *vaqueros* grinned. They had good reason to be proud, Sundance thought. They had come through it alive and not a cow had been lost.

Molly glared at Frank Pendleton when he tried to show her the slight wound he had received. Molly had the kind of fatigue that makes some people look keen-eyed and alert. The others, all but the *vaqueros*, the iron men from the south, were worn out in an ordinary way. Bowdry looked ready to drop.

Frank Pendleton complained to Sundance about Molly's indifference. "It's hard to be a hero, boss. Here I am honorably wounded and she won't even give me a smile."

"She'll cry at your funeral," Bennington said, still a rival for Molly's affections.

"Too bad he wasn't shot in the tongue," Molly said, but without the rancor she had shown the day before. She headed for the post.

Charlie Starbright and the *vaqueros*, the most experienced men in the outfit, stayed with the herd while the others went to eat and sleep for a few hours. Smoke from cookfires spiraled up from the roofs of the buildings as Sundance and Francisco Aldama, with Bennington behind, went down to the river to see how much damage they had done to Macdonald. Three dead horses and four dead men lay in the shallows, and farther down another dead man was snagged by his canvas suspenders on a chunk of driftwood. The snagged suspenders gave the corpse a ludicrous appearance.

They heard someone moaning in the tall yellow grass by the river. A hand came up and then a face, a young face sunbrowned but unlined. Sundance drew his Colt and blew a hole in the face. Then he prodded out the spent cartridge and reloaded. Bennington's face was white.

"Did you have to do that?" he exclaimed.

Sundance holstered his pistol. "Maybe you wanted to ride all over the country looking for the law. Maybe you wanted to wait around for the trial? And maybe he'd get off because he worked for the Indian Ring. They take good care of their killers."

Bennington knew he had talked out of turn, but the shock of the killing made him go on. "I'm not arguing the right of it. But the way you killed him! Like a dog!"

Sundance turned away to look for other bodies in the grass and under the riverbank. "The main thing is, he's dead. You wanted to see the Wild West, Bennington. You just saw it."

Francisco Aldama had absolutely no interest in the dead man. To the old Mexican, the killing was as necessary as keeping a gun well-oiled. It wasn't a matter for debate.

"You think we killed more of them?" Francisco said. "I would like to think we killed more of them."

"So would I," Sundance said. "It's likely some fell in deeper water and got carried away by the current, but it's not worth searching for them.

Macdonald can get new men."

Francisco knew that's what Macdonald would do. "It is regrettable that the moon failed us. I am beginning to think Macdonald will be a hard man to kill."

"We'll just have to keep trying," Sundance said.

Chapter Twelve

They left Doan's crossing and started into the Indian Lands at eight o'clock that morning. Before he waved them off, Doan said he would bury the dead men. Sundance knew he would strip them of their guns and boots and anything else they had before he dumped them in a hole. Some of the men shook hands with Doan; the *vaqueros* didn't, and neither did Francisco Aldama.

Doan warned that there might be trouble when they crossed the Comanche reservation. "What kind of trouble I can't rightly say, not being an Indian. They're supposed to be behaving themself right now and maybe they are. Keep an eye peeled, is what I'm telling you. You may have to part with a few fat beeves to keep them happy."

The morning was hot and bright, few clouds in the sky, when they moved out. Everybody was tired but in good spirits, though they had to cross rough country for most of the day. In the late afternoon, following the main trail north, they sighted a Comanche camp in the distance, and before they had gone far from there a hundred mounted bucks came out to have a look. They didn't ride directly to the herd but blocked the trail about a mile above the cattle. Then they waited in silence for the herd to get close.

"Just keep moving," Sundance said.

When they were less than a hundred yards from the Indians, a subchief rode forward and held up his hand. Finding the trail blocked, the cattle began to turn aside. Sundance called a halt and rode forward with Francisco Aldama. Sundance tried English on the chief, but he didn't understand a word of it. Then they used Spanish and he knew what they were saying, more or less, though his own spoken Spanish was halting and guttural. Sundance noticed that there were two Apches in the band and pegged them for renegades.

The chief wanted a powwow and used the Spanish word *negocio*, meaning business. The chief climbed down and so did they. The chief was big for a Plains Indian, a full six feet in height, still muscular though he wasn't far from fifty. He used sign language to augment his bad Spanish. He talked a lot with his mouth and his hands, but there was no need for any of it. Sundance knew what he wanted, which was anything he could get.

They were intruders, the chief said, and he went on about the slaughter of the buffalo by the white hide-hunters and the hunger and poverty among his people. He himself wanted nothing but peace with the whites, but there were many men in his tribe who did not agree with him. It would be a terrible thing if they were forced to go to war in order to fill their wrinkled bellies. But, he argued, the war talk was strong and he wasn't sure he would be able to avoid bloodshed. If war came it would be terrible and bloody.

Sundance knew what was expected of him and he nodded gravely. There was no way to hurry it. Forced to beg and then to threaten, the Indians were as touchy as old women; a wrong word could set them off, and outnumbered ten to one, it could end only one way.

Sundance said he understood the plight of his Indian brothers. As they could see, he was half Indian himself. He didn't mention the Cheyenne, because Indians so far apart as the Cheyenne and the Comanches would have nothing in common. He said he knew about the hunger of the children and the rumble of empty bellies. However, he did not want to offer the Comanches, all great warriors, the gift of charity but payment for passage across their lands. And what did the chief think would be fair?

Sizing up the herd, the chief said twenty beeves. In Spanish, he said he thought that was more than fair.

"Ten beeves," Sundance stated. Ten beeves and no more.

The chief said he would smoke and think about it. Francisco Aldama passed over rank Mexican tobacco and papers and they all sat on the ground while the chief rolled a smoke. The two Apaches watched.

Ten beeves and no more, Sundance repeated. Francisco told the chief he could keep the tobacco as a gift. Sucking in the bitter smoke, the chief said it was good tobacco. It was too bad he didn't have more for the weeks to come. Francisco agreed but said it was all the tobacco he had.

Ten beeves, Sundance said a third time.

What about coffee? the chief wanted to know.

They had loaded up at Doan's, so there was plenty of coffee. Two sacks of Arbuckle's coffee and two sacks of sugar were fetched from the supply wagon. The chief passed tobacco and paper to the two Apaches. Sundance guessed the squat renegades were the chief's military advisers.

Finally, after much face-saving, the chief agreed to take ten beeves as payment. Francisco told the *vaqueros* to cut out the beeves and to let the Indians have them.

By the time the Indians left it was getting dark, but Sundance told the men to move the herd before they bedded down for the night. The Comanches might get tempted during the night, and a few miles travel might make the difference. So they moved on well past dark and it was close to nine o'clock before the herd was allowed to rest. It rained hard during the night and it was still raining at daybreak when they rolled out and started a new day. The sky was low and gray and the good spirits of the previous day had been washed away by the rain. Molly got a fire going in spite of the driving rain, though it hissed and threatened to go out when the wind gusted hard. The smoke from the fire blew around, blinding them. Bothered by the rain, the cattle bawled. Knocked down by wind and rain, the prairie grass looked as flat and soggy as they felt.

Breakfast over, they headed out under lowering skies and a few hours later, when they struck the Salt Fork River, they found it raging and impassable. There was nothing to do but wait for it to go down, and that killed the rest of the day. It kept on raining until it was dark, then it stopped except for an occasional squall. By daybreak the river had gone down enough to start the herd across.

They got the herd across in about thirty minutes, but it took a good part of the day to move the chuckwagon to the far shore. The still high river was well over a hundred yards wide; most of that was swimming distance. Looking at the current in the river, Sundance said, "Nothing to do but raft the wagon across."

A lot more time was wasted looking for the timber to make the raft, and they had to scout along the Salt Fork for several miles before they found it: dry, dead cottonwood. Then they had to cut it with the two axes they had. Sundance and Frank Pendleton began the cutting and were spelled by the other men as they went along. The *vaqueros* were no good with the axes; Lars Lindermann, from the lumber lands of Sweden, was the best of the lot. Rain gusted now and then but didn't keep up.

The logs were dry and light and they roped them and dragged them down to the river. When all was ready they ran the wagon into two-foot water and built the raft under it. They had cut the logs about twenty feet long and now they ran a tier of them under the wagon between the wheels. These were lashed securely to the axles, after which they made cross timberings and outside guard logs. As they worked the wagon rose on the raft and would have floated away if it hadn't been held there by rope anchors. Six of them rode down into the water, holding on to the heavy tow lines. Then they let the wagon go with the current, guiding it for the far bank. After that, the rest of the crossing was easy.

It rained all night and the men were miserable; trying to stay dry was a waste of time. Sundance didn't try to do any cheering up, for nothing made an angry man madder than to have somebody telling him that things weren't so bad. There still remained the danger of Indian raids and at one point they came to a cross trail that went toward the low sand hills to the east. Because of the rain the tracks of the Indian herd were mostly washed away, but it must have been a stolen herd of considerable size, and not less than fifty horses. During the night a double guard was posted, but the dark hours passed without incident.

By the next afternoon they were well north of the Comanche reservation. All the time they were doing their best to hold to a due north course. It stopped raining and the prairie steamed in the hot sunshine. Then they crossed the North Fork and the South Canadian. At a forlorn army post Molly went in with Charlie Starbright to buy flour and navy beans. They came back and said there were absolutely no eggs, fresh or stale, to be had. The men didn't complain too much about the eggs, because the sun was shining and the sky was thick with fleecy clouds that blew away on the prairie wind.

That night they had a good dry supper and some of the men played poker on a blanket beside a blazing fire. Full of coffee and beans and biscuits, Frank Pendleton went back to the bragging about the fight at Doan's Crossing. Bennington sketched by firelight but he let Molly alone. Charlie Starbright told some of his windy Texas tales, and there was a feeling of good fellowship for the first time in nearly a week. They weren't such a bad bunch, Sundance thought. He had seen a lot worse in his time.

A few days later they would reach the outskirts of Dodge, and that's where he guessed Macdonald had gone to recruit another band of men. Dodge was the only town of any size in this part of the country. The town had pretty good law, thanks to Marshal Matt Dillon; it was wild enough just the same. In the cribs and low saloons there would be hard cases willing to work for Macdonald. Yet it might take a while to round them up, and maybe he should go in there and take a look, for he knew Macdonald might be getting desperate along about now. They had come all the way from Texas, from as far south as you could get, and they hadn't been stopped. The Indian Ring had agents everywhere; they were bound to have a man in a big cowtown like Dodge. If Macdonald failed to get results he would find the Ring agents breathing down his neck, and maybe worse.

"I think you are taking a big chance," Francisco Aldama said when Sundance told him his thoughts. "You face much danger if you go alone. If you leave the herd unguarded you may lose everything. I would like to go with you."

"Can't let you," Sundance said. "If something happens to me you know how to get the herd to Montana. Charlie's a good cowhand but he's light in the head. You stay here and be foreman. Let me take the *vaqueros*. Three good men is all the backing I need."

"Perhaps," the old man said. "They are good men all right, hard as nails, good with their guns. I feel bad that I can't go, but you are the boss."

Sundance smiled at the fierce old fighter. "Cheer up," he said. "My guess is we'll have plenty of fighting before this is over. Call your men now. I'd like to get started."

"I will take the herd well north of the town," Francisco said. "If you don't show up in five days

I don't know what I will do. I may go looking for you."

"No *segundo*," Sundance said. "You will not come looking for me. You will take the herd north to Montana."

"I do not like this," Francisco said. "But I will call the men."

Late on the afternoon of the second day after leaving camp, Sundance and the Mexicans sighted the smoke of passing trains. Jesus, Ramon and Cesar waited impassively for Sundance to give them orders.

"It's about twenty more miles," he said. "But we won't push it. I don't want to get in there too early." Sundance spoke in Spanish, for only Ramon understood English. "Macdonald knows what we look like so he has the advantage there. But I'll know his voice if I hear it again. Will you?"

They nodded. "We heard it at the river," Jesus said. "There is no mistaking it. The others? Who can say what they look like."

"Macdonald is the one we have to get, if we can," Sundance said. "He is the madman, the *loco*."

Cesar never had anything to say, but now he did. "You think maybe we can take him alive?"

Sundance said, "The others wouldn't hold back because we had Macdonald. The feisty ones in his bunch would want us to kill him so they could take over. Maybe you're thinking of torture?"

"Just a little torture," Cesar agreed. "He would suffer less in the next world if he got used to it first."

"Just be glad if you can kill him. We may have to face Matt Dillon and I'd just as soon not have to do that. Anyway, the law hasn't done us any good. Dillon or no Dillon, I'm not going to hang or sit in jail for twenty years."

Ramon said, "That would not be a good idea. But you must tell us what to do. We are strangers here."

Sundance nodded. "You won't stand out too much in Dodge. Lots of Southwest outfits use *vaqueros*. I'm the one that's going to stand out, but there's no help for that. We'll split up when we get there and come in from north and south. Dillon may have a lid on the town because Macdonald is there. All we can do is go there and look."

Traveling easy, they reached Dodge about midnight; the town blazed with light. It lay on the prairie in a pool of light, and when they got closer they could hear the din of the saloons, gaming houses and dance halls. In the corrals on all sides of the railroad yards penned cows, bound for the Chicago meat packers, bawled at the uproar. Sundance had been there before, though never with a herd, and it hadn't changed any. This was a town without roots; of wild young cowboys and grizzled oldtimers; of whores and gamblers—all the flotsam of the frontier. There were plenty of killers in Dodge, but Matt Dillon kept his eye on them, and they were welcome to stay as long as they didn't shoot anyone. Dillon was a good man with a sawed-off shotgun, meaning that he was a very bad man with a sawed-off shotgun. But for a marshal in a wide-open town, Dillon was fair enough, if his own interests weren't threatened. A lot of bad men had tried to kill Dillon, but they were dead and he still was walking around, so that said as much as could be said about the man. Dillon had no leave-your-guns-at-home law. He didn't have to, because only a damn fool dared to shoot out saloon lights in his town. It had a big Boot Hill.

Sundance went in first from the south end of town. Cesar followed him after a time. The other two came in from the north. When Sundance saw some lanky buffalo hunters in buckskins he felt better about it. He looked much the same except that he had copper skin and washed when he could. The whores in the cribs were doing a brisk trade. A tough looking middle-aged deputy with a Winchester carbine stared at him, then went on his way. There were too many wild looking men in town to give him more than the usual attention. He didn't see Dillon but then Dillon spent most of his time in the jail or the Long Branch Saloon playing poker and blackjack. Gamblers who wanted to get on the marshal's good side always let him win reasonable amounts.

Sundance got down and waited for the *vaqueros* to get close to him. They liked all the lights and the loud music. Jesus smiled at a girl on the sidewalk until Ramon, a grave man much older, reminded him what he was there for.

They made their way along the long main street. Other streets ran off it, but they were dark and quiet, filled with frame houses. When they reached the Long Branch, Sundance eased his way to the window and spotted Matt Dillon at a table with his back to the wall, playing poker with five other men. Drinkers stood two-deep at the famous long bar; none looked as if he belonged to Macdonald's bunch.

"We'll check the other places first," Sundance said. "Then we'll come back here. Maybe we can do our business and ride out fast. If we get out fast Dillon won't bother too much about coming after us."

A few minutes later they found the place they were looking for, a single story saloon with about ten horses hitched out in front of it. It didn't have a piano or any of the other noise-makers. A rudely lettered wooden sign advertised big schooners of beer for a nickel. To Sundance it had the look of all the rundown saloons in the world. It was fairly well filled and the murmur of loud conversation drifted out through the open door; when the talk ebbed the slap-slap of cards could be heard.

Moving among the tethered horses Sundance found one, a big brown, with a fancy Mexican saddle. The horse and the saddle had cost money. The brand didn't tell him anything, but it didn't have to be Macdonald inside, because plenty of mounts came up from Old Mexico.

The men playing poker sat at a table under a hanging lantern, and it was hard to see some of their faces. The back door was open for the air and the lantern swung slightly in the breeze, lighting and then shadowing their faces. Then, as he watched, Sundance heard Macdonald's loud, hoarse voice. The Mexicans heard it too, and they tensed. The voice sounded again; Macdonald was losing and not liking it.

Sundance whispered to Ramon and Cesar to go around to the back door. "You heard Macdonald, the big man in the gray Stetson. When I come in shoot him in the back. Then we'll get out fast before Dillon's deputies show up."

"That's the way to do it," Cesar agreed.

Ramon and Cesar went into the alley between the saloon and the next building. Sundance waited with Jesus next to him, holding his drawn pistol against his leg. In the saloon Macdonald bellowed again. Sundance was going in the door when he heard Matt Dillon's voice behind him.

"You going somewhere, Sundance?"

"No Jesus!" Sundance said as the Mexican began to whirl. "Hold your fire!"

"Walk on in," Dillon ordered. "Walk in or get blown in. Nobody's coming in the back door except my deputies. We got to have this out. Fight your war someplace else. Not in my town you don't."

Sundance and Jesus went in with Dillon and three hard-faced deputies behind them. They all had the impersonal eyes of legal killers. The men at the table whirled. Macdonald was reaching for his gun when Dillon pointed the shotgun straight at him.

"Be good," Dillon said quietly as he leveled the shotgun. "Be good or be gone."

Three more deputies came in the back door pushing Ramon and Cesar in front of them. Ramon was bleeding from a blow on the head. "That one objected," one of the shotgun toters said.

Macdonald stood up and Sundance hadn't realized how big he was until then. He must have been six-four and had reddish Scotch hair and fierce blue eyes. His sandy mustache didn't show much against his sun-reddened skin. He wore a dark wool shirt and whipcord pants. Sundance could see his boots but heard the jingle of big Mexican spurs.

"What's going on, Dillon?" Macdonald said, and when the light swung Sundance saw the old bullet wound in his throat. That explained the strange, rasping voice.

Macdonald was a fearsome man but Dillon remained unperturbed. "You just wore out your welcome, Macdonald. I want you gone from Dodge. I want all you fellows gone from Dodge. That includes you and the Mexicans, Sundance. I know the story—I hear everything goes on—and I don't give a damn about the right or wrong of it. Like I said, find another place to fight your war."

Macdonald stared at Dillon, wanting to draw on him, but knowing he'd get blasted from front and back if he did. "We haven't broken any law, Dillon. The halfbreed is the one should be run off, not me."

It looked like Dillon wanted to get back to his poker game. "I'm the law and nobody else," he warned. "Now why don't you just finish your game while your friends here go on their way."

One of the other poker players was very young and very drunk. He stood up and spoke to Macdonald. "You want to take them on, Larch? I feel so good I don't care what I do."

Without turning, Macdonald told him to shut up. "We'll do what you say, Dillon, but not because we're afraid of you."

"Oh go to blazes!" Dillon said. "I'm getting tired of this. Half of you boys stay with Macdonald, the rest of you escort Sundance out of town."

Just then the kid's hand streaked for his gun.

Even if he hadn't been drunk it would have been a good draw. Dillon was half-turned away when it happened. Sundance knew the kid was trying for Dillon, and his own gun came out just a second faster. The kid's gun was out when Sundance's bullet shattered his arm. The gun dropped and he reeled back trying to grab a gun from one of the other men.

"Wait!" Macdonald yelled. "He's drunk, is all!"

"Not good enough!" Dillon said. "Everybody step away from him!" The men close to the kid lurched away from him. The kid's eyes were wide and scared and afraid to die. Dillon brought up the shotgun and blew him off his feet. He hit the wall and slid down it almost cut in two. Nothing else moved as Dillon calmly reloaded.

Dillon didn't look at Sundance. "You shot off a pistol in my town, my friend. Better be on your way before I decide to do something about it. Macdonald and the rest of his bravos are going to jail for a while."

"For how long?" Sundance asked. "I'd kind of like to know."

Macdonald's red face flamed redder. "I'll still stop you, halfbreed. Depend on that!"

Dillon held the shotgun hip high. "You want some of this, Macdonald? You want some, you can have it. I could send you to jail for attempted murder of a police officer, but it's not my custom to burden the taxpayers. I think a week in jail will hold you for a while. You get a week's start, Sundance, but you'll have to pay the cost of feeding these men. I'd say that was a pretty good bargain, don't you?"

Sundance smiled at the venal lawman. "Cheap at the price," he said, handing over the sum of money the marshal named. It was more than he expected. He went out followed by the three Mexicans.

They had a week to make up for lost time.

Chapter Thirteen

They galloped west, picked up the tracks of the herd, and caught up to it before dawn. Dawn came earlier now, and all the days would be long, if they hoped to outdistance Macdonald. Once Dillon let him out of jail, Macdonald would start off like the hammers of hell, taking remounts along so he could travel day and night, driving his men with curses and promises. With Dodge behind them, Sundance and the others had broken the back of the drive; they were well over halfway. On the plains of northwest Kansas wood for cooking was going to be scarce, but they would halt only when they had to and stay there the shortest possible time. Yet they couldn't drive the herd too hard, or there would be a lot of cow skulls along the trail. All they could do was move on and make the best of it.

As the country dried out under the sun it lost its green look of spring and turned brown. It was flat and monotonous, broken only by mirages. In the distance, a running antelope would look twenty times its normal size. From the mirages came the danger of a stampede, but the herd continued to move at a steady pace. There was no wood and Molly used buffalo chips for what cooking she did. They crossed into Nebraska, though the country remained absolutely the same: flat, dull and hot.

Wyoming lay ahead; soon they would be at the end of the line, if they got that far. Larch Macdonald was in all their thoughts. The week had passed and they knew he was on his way. Sundance made a number of plans and discarded all of them. He knew he would have to find something better to stop Macdonald when he came. If they reached Montana they could count on help from the Cheyenne, though he didn't want to involve the Cheyenne in the killing of whites for any reason. But he would have to do what was needed to be done when the time came.

They had to cross a long, absolutely waterless fifty miles to reach the South Platte. By bedding the herd during the day and watering, they were able to get to water the following morning. The cows bawled at being moved at night. To save time they gave the wild town of Ogallala a miss, and kept going. Sundance had been thinking about Ogallala. There wasn't a church in the whole town, though that wasn't what concerned him. There was a telegraph line in Ogallala; it was possible that Macdonald had wired ahead from Dodge.

From where they were camped for the short night they could see the lights of the town. The first watch was quiet but when it was time for the second one Jules Bowdry was missing. Molly came over to listen to Charlie Starbright telling Sundance, and when she heard the news she looked startled and headed for the chuckwagon. Without a word she checked her pistol and began to saddle a horse from the *remuda*. Sundance came up fast and caught the bridle before she could ride out. She tried to kick at him, but he yanked her from the saddle.

Francisco Aldama came to report that Bowdry was nowhere in or around the camp.

"Where do you think you're going?" Sundance asked Molly, who was struggling.

She kicked at him. "Bowdry ran off with something that belongs to me. Don't ask what. It's none of your business. I have to get it back."

Now and then Sundance had thought about the carpetbag that Molly watched so carefully. It hadn't mattered until now. "What is it?" he said roughly.

"None of your business, I said."

"Then it doesn't matter. We'll let the gambler go."

"Like hell you will. You can't keep me here."

"You signed on for the trip. We need a cook."

Molly's temper flared again. "You make me go without my property I'll poison the lot of you. You specially. I'll feed you ground glass that'll cut up your guts."

Francisco stepped forward with a thin smile on his leathery face. "Sundance, I think she means it. I can't see dying that way."

Molly kicked at Sundance again. "I'll ruin the food and run off every chance I get."

"We have till morning to find the gambler. I think the young lady's property was too great a temptation for him. Fear and temptation combined to make him run. He was the only one who was afraid all the time. I could see it," said the old Mexican.

Sundance held the girl. "I saw it too, but he fought well enough. And maybe it's possible that he was a spy for Macdonald but lost his nerve. Now he's afraid that Macdonald will catch up with him."

"That could be," Francisco said. "He saw the young lady's property as a way out. Now we must go quickly and find him."

Sundance pushed Molly away from the horse, but she ran back to it. "I'm coming too. He took what's mine so I'm coming too."

Francisco shrugged at Sundance. "Why not? This time I am coming with you."

"If you want," Sundance said. "But find him or not, we're going to be back here to move the herd at dawn. You'll be here too, Molly, if I have to tie you up between meals. We'll check in Ogallala but he may have headed on to the railroad stop at Big Springs."

It was still fairly early when they turned away from the river and rode into Ogallala a few hundred yards away. The South Platte ran west, then south into Colorado. The train stop at Big Springs was about twenty miles away. Sundance didn't know this country all that well. There might be another, closer train station at a village called Brule. He wasn't sure.

At the depot in Ogallala Bowdry was nowhere in sight and the sleepy station agent said he hadn't seen anybody who looked like that. "Train will be along in about an hour," the station man told them. "Won't be another train till morning."

They went outside and Sundance said, "If he's hiding out there in the dark he'll stay in cover. Wait for the morning train or just ride out and hope to make it that way. If he is there and we leave maybe he'll get on the train. If he's on the train we'll catch him at the next stop."

Francisco sighed. "Perhaps never."

"I'll catch him," Molly raged. "The sneaking son of a bitch!"

Sundance stared at her. "What the hell is in that bag? Somebody's family silver?"

"Never you mind, foreman."

"It's making a lot of trouble."

"Maybe it'll be worth it. If he's working—was working—for Macdonald he'll tell you a lot of things."

Francisco touched the silver-handled knife on his belt. "He'll tell and be glad to tell."

They mounted up and headed back for the river and when they got there they followed the curve of the railroad tracks where they ran along the north bank. Eighteen miles was good going for a horse at night, even if they were pushing it and there was a moon. The tracks and the river and the road all ran in the same direction. Despite his age, Francisco rode effortlessly, enjoying the wild journey. The wind had pushed up the old man's floppy hat and there was a wild look in his eyes. Molly, thinking of her carpetbag, rode just as fiercely. Sundance wondered if they would find Bowdry; if they would get anything out of him if they *did* find him. The man might just be a cheap thief.

The small depot at Brule had been boarded up and abandoned, with no way to stop the train when it came. They rode on covering the dark miles to Big Springs. The lights of the village were in sight when they heard the hooting of the train far behind them. Sundance turned and saw the big light of the locomotive shafting through the darkness. Sundance touched Eagle's flank with his heels and the big stallion surged ahead of the others. He covered the last two miles well ahead of them and beat the train into the depot. Two men and a child were waiting for the train and they looked at him curiously as he jumped down and ran to the train pulling in with clanging bells and explosions of steam. He climbed up past the startled conductor and started through the cars.

Jules Bowdry was in the second car with his hat tilted over his eyes, Molly's carpetbag between his feet. Sundance came silently on moccasined feet and stood over him. Bowdry sensed his presence and pushed the hat back, his other hand reaching half-heartedly for his gun. Sundance reached out with iron fingers and took it away from him.

"Trip's been canceled, Jules," he said, pulling Bowdry to his feet. "Pick up the bag and walk out ahead of me. Don't make a fuss and scare the passengers."

Mumbling something, Bowdry climbed down from the train. The conductor, about to call "all aboard!" asked why the gentleman was getting off and Sundance said the gentleman had changed his mind. He didn't want a charge of kidnaping or train robbing or whatever it was.

"Suit yourself," the conductor said, slamming the door.

Jules Bowdry gave the train a despairing look as it pulled out. Francisco and Molly were waiting on lathered horses. Sundance thought the old man's face looked very cruel; the wild look hadn't left his eyes.

With Bowdry mounted up behind the girl, they started back for camp. Bowdry tried to talk but Sundance warned him to be quiet. "You'll get a chance to talk and you better think about it. Lie and I'll let the Mexicans have you."

Bowdry carried Molly's carpetbag all the way back, but he held it as a man might hold a rattlesnake by the back of the head. Sundance wanted to give his imagination time to work. Most men lost confidence when they had too much time to think. They rode in silence along the river, then past the still brawling town.

Everybody was waiting when they rode in; the herd was quiet. "So you caught the blackguard," Frank Pendleton said, grinning up at the gambler. "What did Molly have that was so precious?"

It would be dawn in an hour and Sundance didn't want to waste any time. He pulled Bowdry down from the horse and pushed him over by the fire. "Now everybody be quiet. I'm going to say a few things to this man and don't want any tough talk or smart talk. All right, Bowdry, listen to me. I think you started out as a paid spy for Macdonald and got nervous about it. You didn't do what you were paid to do, so you kept looking for a way out. You couldn't run out in Dodge because that's where Macdonald was. Ogallala was the first chance you got. Molly had something you could spend or sell. Nobody's asking you what it was. I want to know about Macdonald."

Bowdry turned sullen eyes on Molly. "Did she make up that story about Macdonald? Well, she's nothing but a thief. That bag of hers is stuffed with a whole bunch of money and gold certificates made out to some man in Galveston, Texas. Why don't you ask her about that?"

Sundance slapped the tinhorn in the mouth so hard he knocked him over. Then he dragged him back to a sitting position. Molly, clutching the bag, remained silent.

"I'm asking you about Macdonald," Sundance said. "What Molly did or didn't do doesn't matter a damn. Let me explain how it is. It's kind of one-sided. If you say you aren't, I won't believe you. Tell me you are, and I will. But you'll have to make it good. Tell me some things I have to know."

Bowdry gave himself a minute to think. "What if I tell you I'm not? You don't have the reputation of torturing men."

Francisco Aldama smiled and took out his silver-handled stabbing knife. "I'm not half so noble, my friend."

Sundance let the gambler see how the knife glinted in the firelight. It was double-edged, as sharp as a razor. "Once he starts he won't stop for a while," Sundance said. "You're not tough enough to take it. No man is, least of all you."

Sundance looked up at the sky. It was turning gray. Guarded by the last watch, the herd was stirring. "I won't waste any more time with you," Sundance said. "You'll stay behind with Francisco. You'll be screaming by sunup."

The knife was still in the old man's hands. He turned the blade in the yellow light.

Bowdry watched it and licked his lips. "What happens if I tell the truth? You'll just kill me."

Sundance had been thinking about it. It was better to make a deal with the man and to stick with it. "Wrong," he said. "You have my word on that. You know me so you know it's good. For the last time, what about Macdonald?"

Bowdry tried not to look at the knife, yet it fascinated him. Bowdry said, "It started like I told you. I was down and out in Brownsville. I guess they were looking for men willing to do anything for money. I was. Listen to me, I don't even know what Macdonald looks like. It wasn't him that approached me. One of his men. Jones he said he was."

Francisco sneered. "Mr. Smith Jones. Tell the truth, *ladron*—thief!"

"Let him talk," Sundance said.

Bowdry stared at Sundance, trying to find reassurance in his stony face. "Jones he said he was. He gave me a hundred dollars to get a job with the outfit. To ride along to see what happened. I was mostly drunk when I took the money. I lost most of it at roulette, drank up the rest the day before you got to Brownsville. This Jones found me drunk the day you went to the bartender, Paddy. He said there was a job waiting I better take."

"*Embustero!*" Francisco said. "He is a liar!"

Sundance glanced at the old man. His face was white and angry, very tired.

"Go on, Bowdry," he said.

"I went to Paddy and he told me to do what Jones said, or they'd kill me. So I did, figuring I could lose myself along the trail."

Sundance asked, "What were you supposed to do? Feed jimson weed to the cows?"

Bowdry shook his head. "I didn't do that. All Jones gave me was the money and two names. If you—we—got as far as Dodge, I was to find a way to talk to a man named Atwood, a lawyer, and tell him what you were saying, what you were planning. Maybe you know him?"

"I know who he is. Handles crooked lawsuits for the Indian Ring. What was the other name?"

"Barnes, also in Dodge, a big businessman."

Sundance nodded. "Know his name too. What made you change your mind, Bowdry?"

Bowdry looked around at the circle of faces in the firelight. "I just wanted no part of it. I'm a broken-down gambler, not a hard case or hired gun. But that wasn't the real reason. On the way here I got to know some of you pretty well. I couldn't tell you the truth, so I just tried to get out."

Francisco slapped the flat of the blade against the palm of his left hand. "So you stole the girl's bag and left us to die!"

Bowdry answered the old man without looking at him. "She's no better than me."

"*Culebra*! Snake!" The angrier the old man got, the more he lapsed into Spanish. Francisco had grown fond of Molly. "She is not like you! She is a decent girl and she has been loyal all the way. What she is not, dead man, is a spy like you."

Sundance wished Francisco would shut up. "Jones, so-called, must have told you a few things?"

Bowdry said, "He did. He figured I was too scared to talk. He said Macdonald was going to keep you busy all along the trail, but the real final attack was going to come when you crossed the Montana line into Cheyenne territory. Jones said that would be Macdonald's big revenge for what happened to his family years ago. Indians would starve and Macdonald would laugh."

Sundance pictured the country to the north in his head. The most frequently used, the easiest trail from Wyoming and the south, crossed the Montana border through a long brushy, wooded canyon with sheer walls on both sides. A good clear trail ran through, but if both ends were sealed off there was absolutely no way out. He knew where it was and he had been through it many times, as boy and man. Even an agile man would find it hard to scale the red walls of Neely's Canyon. He spoke the name of the place to Bowdry. "Was that it?"

Bowdry's frantic eyes showed some real hope for the first time. "You know it, so you know I'm telling the truth. You know the names of the men in Dodge. Now you know what's waiting for you at the end."

Sundanced thought he knew. "He plans to burn the whole herd alive in there. Block the far end, then set the whole thing ablaze from end to end. Right within a day's drive of where the cows are supposed to go."

Listening to Sundance Bowdry became almost confident. "And I'm the one told you his plan."

Before Sundance could make a move the knife had flashed from the old man's hand and buried itself in Bowdry's throat. Blood bubbled up, and his hands raised up and cut themselves on the double edges in their efforts to get it out. His eyes opened wide, staring at Sundance in horrified reproach. Then he sagged forward and died.

Sundance turned and Francisco's old face was still defiant, the eyes still angry. It was hard to surprise Sundance—but he was surprised.

"Say nothing to me," Francisco said. "He deserved to die and I killed him. I would kill him again. You had no right to promise him his freedom."

"I had the right and you know it. What's wrong with you? Why did you do this stupid thing?"

Red spots burned in the old man's sickly face

and his hand went close to his gun. "You call me stupid, you bastard Indian!"

Bowdry's corpse twitched in the firelight. No one gave it any attention. Sundance's face had gone tight with unaccustomed anger, but it faded as the old man began to fall. He grabbed him with both hands and set him down gently. The three *vaqueros* came over and stood waiting.

"What is this?" Sundance asked.

Ramon answered. "You are his good friend, so there is no disgrace in the telling. Don Francisco is very much afraid of death."

"What're you saying? He's one of the bravest men I know. It can't be that."

"It is," Ramon went on. "He is afraid to die naturally. A bullet or a knife would mean nothing to him. That is how he wants to die—quickly! But the failing of his body—his heart—terrifies him. His heart is diseased so he fears death by heart failure. It has troubled him for many years. He thinks to die like that is not to die like a man. The fear makes him angry, sad, maybe crazy. Yes, I think crazy! Do not be angry with him, because he is a good and great man. We all fear something that drives us crazy."

Fetching a rolled-up blanket, Molly made a pillow for the old man's head. She covered him with another blanket. She called his name, but he didn't answer.

"Oh God!" she said.

"I will get the brandy for him," Jesus said. "Tonight he dared his diseased heart by riding too much. I think he will die now."

Holding the brandy close to the old man's mouth, Molly poured a trickle between his teeth after she forced them open with her fingers, and in a while he began to cough. Molly waited before she gave him a lot more brandy.

"Not so much," Ramon warned.

The old man's eyes fluttered open and he stared wildly, hardly knowing where he was.

Sundance stopped beside him. "You're all right, Francisco. You're not dead—just a little crazy. And now a little crazy with good strong brandy."

The *vaqueros* dared to smile, but were nervous about it. Sundance waved them to take away Bowdry's body. Suddenly, the old man remembered what he had done and he stiffened with shock. He covered his face with his hand.

"Oh that name I called you, Sundance." Nothing was said about the cold-blooded murder of Jules Bowdry. "Take my pistol and kill me like a man. Put an end to my worthless life. Go on—do it!"

Sundance said, "Don't be so dramatic, Francisco. You did worse than call me names. Hell, I don't care that much about Bowdry, but I hoped to get more out of him. You spoiled that, you silly old bastard!"

Francisco propped himself up on an elbow and felt his chest with his fingers. "My heart doesn't sound too bad. Maybe I won't die tonight after all."

"Not unless I kill you," Sundance said. "You want to walk or be carried? We have to get moving."

Three days later they were in sight of Neely's Canyon.

Chapter Fourteen

Lying in thick brush on top of the long ridge, Sundance caught the tiny flash of sun on field glasses. He was able to use his own glasses without danger of being seen because he and Francisco were in shadow and the watcher on top of the great bulk of the canyon wall was directly in the light of the setting sun. No more sun flashes came from the great red wall facing them miles away. One was all they needed to know that Macdonald and his men were up there. It couldn't be a hunter, because this was desolate country long hunted out by the Indians. And to kill the game that was left a man didn't need field glasses.

Francisco used the glasses and handed them back to Sundance. "I will take your word. I didn't see anything," the old Mexican said.

Sundance said, "They saw all they needed to know, the herd bedding down for the night. It's natural for us to start the cows toward the canyon at first light. What else would we do!"

The dying sun washed everything in brown-red light. For some people this would be the quietest time of the day, to ease the muscles after work, to look forward to supper. But up there on the canyon wall men were waiting to destroy them.

old man frowned. "But what if they set the

fires in the night? Or have set them already? We could walk into a trap of our own making."

Sundance glassed what he could see of the canyon; not much light was left. "Not too likely," he said. "They'll be using coal oil to soak the brush and grass. If they did that at night, hours before we move, it wouldn't have the same effect. I'm betting they'll do it as soon as the herd starts to move. When they see it move they'll come down from the heights to the floor of the canyon and do their work. We have to be in the high places when they climb down. As soon as they're finished I start loosing the fire arrows."

Francisco argued about catching all of the raiders. "If the other end of the canyon isn't blocked some—maybe all—could get away."

Sundance looked at the old man. "If you wanted to cremate three-thousand cows, what would you do?"

Francisco shrugged an end to his argument. "I would block the other end of the canyon."

"You'd block it good and tight," Sundance said. "Barricade it with dead trees and piled-up brush. On both sides of the trail the brush and trees run right up high on the canyon walls. Above that it's sheer rock. It isn't that wide a trail, so locked in like that it'll be like trying to escape from one big red-hot skillet. Macdonald and his boys will fry like steaks."

The old man smiled an evil smile. "I like that description. This man has given us so much trouble, has caused so much pain. Think of it, he will burn tomorrow and forever in hell." A frown creased Francisco's sunbrowned forehead. "There could be trouble with the herd. It has to be taken fairly close to the mouth of the canyon, or Macdonald will suspect something."

"Not too close," Sundance said. "Close enough. The men will have to work like hell to control them. Sometimes when cows see any big opening they run toward it. You want to stay with the herd or come with me?"

Sundance looked away from Francisco because he began to tremble with excitement. "You would take me?" he asked. "You didn't want to take me to Dodge to face the killers."

Sundance turned back to look at him. "I figure I owe you this. We're so close to where we're going, there won't be any more excitement once we're through the pass. You're a bad old man to want excitement so much." Sundance smiled. "But I know how you feel."

Francisco's excitement passed and was replaced by worry. "But what if I should fail you in the morning? We can't take anyone else. If I fail you, then you will have to do it by yourself."

"I could fail *you*," Sundance said. "Then you would have to do it. When it's time, all you do is light the fire arrows and shoot them all over the place. Mostly right along the trail. They'll have fire arrows ready—bet on it."

"My old arms are not that strong."

"You shoot some, I'll shoot the rest. We'll get it done. There's no way to miss. It's all straight down, hundreds of feet of nothing but rockface to the bottom. It's been dry for a month. The whole canyon will go whomp!"

"A nice sound!" the old man said.

It was nearly dark when they edged down off the slope and went back to camp. The herd was bedded and in good shape. Everyone except the first watch was waiting by the fire. It was a big fire, to make it look good. They all knew what was ahead, but there was no sign of nervousness. They had come too far, had crossed the entire United States in the face of too much danger, to be nervous now. Sketch pad on his knee, Bennington was making yet another charcoal drawing of Charlie Starbright.

In not too many sentences, Sundance told them what he and the old man were going to do. There was dead silence for a moment, then he continued.

"The whole thing will go wrong if you don't keep a tight hold on the herd. If you don't, Macdonald will have done what he set out to do. With help from us. They'll watch you for a while to make sure you're heading the right way. Maybe they won't all go down to the canyon floor. Most will have to—it's a big, long canyon—and they'll want to do it right. Francisco and I will have to deal with anybody still up there. When you start you'll have to do it the regular way, and you'll have to keep doing it for at least a mile. The smoke from the canyon will come fast and there will be a lot of it. Black and oily. Barrels of coal oil. The minute you see that turn the herd, scatter it out if you have to. But don't let it head for the valley. Cows in front will be forced inside and the rest will pile up. That's about everything. Anybody got anything to say?"

Nobody except Molly had anything to say and she waved Sundance away from the rest of them. They stood by the chuckwagon in the half-darkness, the light from the fire playing on their faces. Molly was a good-looking woman in any light, Sundance thought. She had washed her spun gold hair and it smelled of yellow soap and hadn't completely dried yet.

Molly said at last and not in her usual defiant voice, "I could go with you and the old man. I'm not that good with the cows. Don Francisco is so old—why are you taking him?"

"Because he wants to go."

"That's no reason."

"Sure it is."

"I think he'd like to get killed tomorrow." She pointed into the darkness. "Up there on that rimrock. Go out in glory!"

"What if he does, if that's what he wants. Don't argue about it. I'm taking him and I'm not taking you."

"Because I'm a woman?"

"Because you're needed with the herd. Every rider has to count."

"That's not the real reason you won't take me. It's because of Don Francisco. If I came along that would make him less of a man."

"I suppose to him it would. Look, Molly, no offense to you but we have to be going."

Molly put her hand on his arm. "You don't care at all about me, do you? All the other men do."

Sundance took her arm away. "I like you fine. This isn't the time."

She got close again. "Will there ever be?"

"Not very likely. You're going on to British Columbia and I'll be heading for Texas. If you're looking for a man, Frank there isn't so bad if you can get used to his dumb jokes. He might settle down. With you he might. Then there's Bennington. Not bad looking, a decent man of his kind, and he'll be well off in a few years. Famous too, unless I miss my guess."

Molly hauled off and whacked Sundance in the face. "Damn you, big man! Don't you make fun of me."

Sundance felt his face; Molly had a good right. "It was just a little fun."

Suddenly she reached out to touch his smarting jaw. "I know it was and I'm sorry I did. You're not even curious about that money, are you?"

Sundance shrugged. "Not much. I guess you worked hard enough to steal it."

"That's not a nice thing to say but that's how I got it. I stole it from a rich old man in Galveston who brought me down there to cook for him. An old man, originally Canadian, like me. I just wanted the job, but he wanted more. He didn't get; he got took away from. I figured the herd was the surest way to get back home without being hunted by the law."

Sundance grinned. "You should write a stern letter to that bartender."

"Maybe I'll do that," Molly said, grinning too. "You ever get up British Columbia way?"

"To buy horses I do. Now and then. A friend of mine, a general in the army, sends me up there to buy English cavalry mounts for breeding. I guess I could make another trip pretty soon. But I warn you, I'll be flat broke after this trip."

Molly kissed him quickly and pulled away. "No, you won't be broke. You'll have a rich women for a friend. No more cooking for this girl. But I will fry a thick steak for you. . .and that's not all I'll do for you."

Sundance stood looking after her. Then he put Charlie Starbright in charge of the outfit and gave him the money to pay off the men, if something happened in the morning. After that they all came to shake his hand, to say goodbye. Even the *vaqueros* came. And then it was time to go.

Francisco picked up the ash bow Sundance had made for him and they started out on foot. Sundance's own bow and quiver of steel-tipped arrows were slung over his shoulder. The arrowheads had been wrapped in rags, a tail left out to keep the flame alight, and soaked for hours in a mixture of gun oil and coal oil. The gun oil would keep the coal oil from drying out. They were going on foot because there would be no place to hide their horses in the morning. The canyon wall that faced the herd fell down to the bottom without a fissure or a hollow place, and at the bottom there were hardly any brush or trees on that side.

The light of the campfire faded behind them and there was the good smell of fat cows on the night wind. No moon showed as they crossed the three miles of flat country between the herd and the mouth of the canyon. As they got closer the canyon wall loomed up tall and massive in the darkness. Setting their pace, they could see the top of the great wall but not the mouth of the canyon that split it as if by the mouth of a gigantic axe. Sundance had glassed the wall for a climbing place before the light was gone. He guessed Macdonald and his men had come there from the north side of the canyon, leaving their horses in a safe place, well tethered. It was easier to get to the top from the north side; there was no hope of doing that, because they would have to traverse the length of the canyon. There might be guards on the canyon floor, posted to take care of any strangers who came from either direction.

Sundance carried a coiled rope on his other shoulder. He wasn't even sure that he could get the old man to the top. But he would try to do it because he owed him this last gesture of friendship. It was unlikely that he would see Francisco Aldama again after the next few days. If he lived he would return to Mexico and disappear into the mists of memory, like so many old friends who were dead. If he couldn't get Francisco to the top, then he would be forced to do it all himself. But he knew he would try very hard to get him there.

No sound but the wind came from the rimrock. Sundance looked up and saw nothing but the lighter black of the night sky. After reaching the side of the wall, it took them fifteen minutes to reach the climbing place. They stopped and listened before they went ahead.

A sliver of moon showed in the dark sky and Sundance felt his way into the crack in the rock. It wasn't more than the width of three men and it didn't run all the way to the bottom. Sundance climbed up first and reached down for the old man's frail wrists. Weapons clacked against rock as he came up. They stood together in the crack, counting off a full minute before they began to feel their way up.

It was easy at first because the crack ran upward at a slant with steps in the rocks. They got up almost a hundred feet without having to climb too hard, then there were no more steps for another twenty feet and Sundance had to leave the old man while he braced his back against one side, his feet against the other, and climbed up that way. There the steps began again and he could free his hands to drop down the rope. In a minute, the old man hissed that he was ready to be drawn up.

The old man was slightly built, but he was all dead weight, about a hundred and thirty pounds of it. It was a chilly night but Sundance was soaked in sweat by the time the old man was dangling a few feet below. Then, after resting, he gave a mighty heave and the old man was drawn up to safety. They rested again, Sundance holding the old man in place, and then climbed again. Inch by inch, they clawed their way to the top. It took them more than ninety minutes to go up nearly four hundred feet.

At the top they lay on a flat rock screened by rabbitbrush. Big sagebrush grew beyond the brush and past that the top of the pass was dotted with white alders and red firs. Rocks were scattered between the trees, plenty of cover for them, or for men who might be waiting for them. They gave it ten minutes before they crawled away from the rim on their bellies. Up there it was cold in the wind and they could see their own campfires miles away on the flat. They crawled on again until they were fairly close to where the rock dropped off into the canyon. There they waited in a hollow sandy place half covered by an overhanging rock.

While they waited they heard them. At first it was quiet except for the wind, then voices came on the wind. There was no way to tell how many men were out there, lying or crouched above the rim of the canyon. They wouldn't have hauled the coal oil barrels to the top, Sundance knew. They'd be on the canyon floor covered by brush and leaves. He thought he heard Macdonald's hoarse voice, but couldn't be sure. Waiting, Sundance thought it was strange how a man's hate could bring him so far, over so many miles for so many years. He understood something about Macdonald's hate, yet he had to destroy him before he did more evil.

During the cold, windy night some man came out of concealment and walked around in the darkness yawning and grunting. It didn't sound like Macdonald. Boots scraped on rock as he came close and he muttered as he pissed only twenty feet away. Maybe he was a Mexican pistolero far from home; from his grunting, it was impossible to say what he was. After he got through, he went away, and then there was nothing but the gritty wind and the high country cold.

Sundance didn't sleep and he didn't let the old man sleep. Francisco was old and he might babble in his dreams. They hadn't brought any water or food. The night wore on and first light began to paint the sky with red. Just before it did, one of the men crawled along the rim of the canyon from where he could see the herd when it began to move. The other men stayed where they were; nothing happened for several minutes. Then there was a series of low whistles and they began to move toward the north end, where they could climb down onto the floor. The man watching the movement of the herd stayed where he was.

The scout lay behind a rock screen by brush, with his hat off. The hat and his rifle lay beside him in the dry dirt. Sundance eased up and ran from rock to rock, like a zigzaging Apache. Shale covered the top of the rock and his feet made scuffing sounds as he ran. He was still nearly forty feet away when the scout jerked around and grabbed for his rifle. His mouth opened to yell and it stayed open, making no sound, when the big

Bowie knife streaked from Sundance's hand and plowed through his heart to the hilt. Sundance ran to get the knife, wiping it quickly. Turning, he waved the old man forward.

Together, they crawled on their bellies to the edge of the rimrock and watched the canyon floor far below. Morning light hadn't fully penetrated the canyon yet. It lay half-black, half-red, the wind blowing through the great mass of trees and brush on both sides of the trail. Sounds of steel barrels being rolled or dragged echoed faintly from below. Sundance waved the old man away from him toward the south end of the canyon. He took the north end where he hoped the opening was securely blocked by a mass of dead, dry trees fronted by brush. The light came up strong like light in a theater.

It got stronger and wasn't so red now. God! There must have been twenty-five of them down there, splashing coal oil into buckets. They ran along both sides of the trail splashing everything like madman. As they emptied the barrels they rolled them off the trail and far back into the trees. Then they emptied all the buckets and threw them as far as they could against the canyon wall. Some were rubbing their hands on their trousers.

Squinting in the morning sunglare, Sundance at last saw the barrier of trees and brush. It was piled up for fifteen feet, blocking the north end of the canyon. Even without a fire, it would have been hard for a man to get over it. He tensed when he spotted Macdonald coming out from under a tree with an empty bucket. Macdonald was careful to shake out every drop of coal oil before he threw away the bucket. Sundance's hands itched to draw a bead on the big Canadian in the gray Stetston and dark shirt. But the barricade had to come first. They would run that way because their horses were somewhere on the other side of it.

Edging his way a little closer, Sundance saw the stack of fire arrows and bows in a crack in the rocks. Macdonald was talking to the men and pointing back up the rimrock. Sundance slithered back from the edge and opened a silver tinderbox. He touched it to the arrowhead and it flared instantly. A thin spiral of spoke went up from it. He turned quickly and nodded at the old man and began to fit an arrow to his bow.

Propping the first flaming arrow over the edge of a rock, Sundance let it burn while he lit the second one. He looked back at the old man, who was too busy to notice him. Here goes whomp! Sundance thought.

He raised up and drew back the huge ash bow and let fly straight and true at the barricade hundreds of feet below. He lit another and loosed it. He did it so fast that the two thocking sounds came almost together. Francisco fired his first arrow while Sundance was loosing the third. From below wild yelling started. Gunfire echoed as they fired up at them, bullets whanging off rocks at the top. As one arrow followed another the whole canyon became a huge sheet of flame. The gunfire kept on for a while, but the raiders were running for their lives.

Sundance kept loosing fire arrows until the quiver was empty. Then he picked up Macdonald's arrows and used them until they were gone. Even at four hundred feet up he felt the force of the inferno below. He saw Macdonald running with his clothes blazing on his feet. He ran until he fell and then there was the second whomping sound—the firestorm in which absolutely nothing can live. Far down from him the old man was standing on the edge of the rim with his hands raised above his head, yelling something that couldn't be heard above the titanic roar of the white firestorm flames. Sundance yelled at him to get back from the edge. Then the wild old Mexican turned to wave one last farewell before he jumped over the edge, turning over and over as he plunged four hundred feet to the bottom.

Sundance, sickened by so much death, turned his back on the man-made hell. He didn't want to see anymore. It was time to get away from there. Nothing would ever be found of Francisco, nothing would be found of any of them; the fire was too fierce for even bones to survive. They would burn to fine dust and blow away on the wind. They would have to rest the herd for a full day before the canyon cooled off enough to take the cows through. They had come a long way, and some had perished on the way; that was how life worked, and there was no getting away from it.

Sundance walked back to the place where they had climbed up and stood looking at the herd scattered all over the flatlands below. They were scattered far and wide, but it wouldn't take that much work to round them up. And when they were ready to travel again, they would take them north to the Cheyenne villages, where the hungry children waited. He didn't feel bad about Francisco Aldama, for he had lived a man's life and died a man's death when the time came. The oily black smoke from the fire rose up into the clear blue sky, and would block it out for a time. But the wind blew everything away, just as life blew people away. The herd looked peaceful on the plain; he felt something close to peace himself. It was over at last.

Sundance went down to meet his friends.

THE MARAUDERS
Peter McCurtin
(Sundance Series)

PRICE: $1.75 LB739
CATEGORY: Western

Blond-haired, copper-skinned Jim Sundance, the halfbreed hero of the prairies, takes on the job of sheriff of Cimarron City when an Indian friend of his is murdered. But Sam Ryker, a powerful cattleman, aimed to take over the town and he wasn't going to let any halfbreed wearing a tin star get in his way. With Ryker's men gunning for him, once again Sundance stands alone!